P9-DCY-910
3 1265 01601 8311

OFFICIALLY
WITHDRAWN

Mar 2018

Ivy Aberdeen's
LETTER *to the*
WORLD

Ivy Aberdeen's
Letter *to the*
World

Ashley Herring Blake

PALATINE PUBLIC LIBRARY DISTRICT
700 N. NORTH COURT
PALATINE, ILLINOIS 60067-8159

LITTLE, BROWN AND COMPANY

New York Boston

This book is a work of fiction. Names, characters, places, and incidents are the product of the author's imagination or are used fictitiously. Any resemblance to actual events, locales, or persons, living or dead, is coincidental.

Copyright © 2018 by Ashley Herring Blake

Cover art copyright © 2018 by Good Wives and Warriors
Cover design by Sasha Illingworth
Cover copyright © 2018 by Hachette Book Group, Inc.

Hachette Book Group supports the right to free expression and the value of copyright. The purpose of copyright is to encourage writers and artists to produce the creative works that enrich our culture.

The scanning, uploading, and distribution of this book without permission is a theft of the author's intellectual property. If you would like permission to use material from the book (other than for review purposes), please contact permissions@hbgusa.com. Thank you for your support of the author's rights.

Little, Brown and Company
Hachette Book Group
1290 Avenue of the Americas, New York, NY 10104
Visit us at LBYR.com

First Edition: March 2018

Little, Brown and Company is a division of Hachette Book Group, Inc.
The Little, Brown name and logo are trademarks of Hachette Book Group, Inc.

The publisher is not responsible for websites (or their content) that are not owned by the publisher.

Library of Congress Cataloging-in-Publication Data
Names: Blake, Ashley Herring, author.
Title: Ivy Aberdeen's letter to the world / Ashley Herring Blake.
Description: First edition. | New York : Little, Brown and Company, 2018. |
Summary: "Twelve-year-old Ivy Aberdeen's house is destroyed in a tornado, and in the aftermath of the storm, she begins to develop feelings for another girl at school." —Provided by publisher.
Identifiers: LCCN 2017019242| ISBN 9780316515467 (hardcover) | ISBN 9780316515498 (ebook) | ISBN 9780316515481 (library edition ebook)
Subjects: | CYAC: Family life—Fiction. | Friendship—Fiction. | Artists—Fiction. | Lesbians—Fiction. | Coming out (Sexual orientation)—Fiction. | Tornadoes—Fiction.
Classification: LCC PZ7.1.B58 Iv 2018 | DDC [Fic]—dc23
LC record available at https://lccn.loc.gov/2017019242

ISBNs: 978-0-316-51546-7 (hardcover), 978-0-316-51549-8 (ebook)

Printed in the United States of America

LSC-C

10 9 8 7 6 5 4 3 2 1

This one is for me.

This is my letter to the world,
that never wrote to me...

—Emily Dickinson

-‹‹‹◆›››-

CHAPTER ONE

Stormy

A storm was coming, which was perfect.

Thunder rumbled through the night, rattling Ivy Aberdeen's bedroom windows and making a beautiful racket. She smiled and counted, only making it to two before lightning washed her room white. Ivy didn't know why people colored bolts of lightning yellow in drawings. They were silvery blue and made her think of whispers and magic, the perfect setting for what Ivy was about to do.

She adjusted the headlamp around her forehead, the thick elastic band pulling at her hair. On her nightstand, her clock glowed green, the numbers already inching toward the time she had to get up for school, but she had a good hour at least. She rubbed the sleep from her eyes, and the tiny headlamp shined a yellow circle onto the notebook in her lap. She called it a notebook because there wasn't a better word for it. She could call it a *journal*, but that didn't feel right either. The book was more like a portable, papery hope chest.

Mom stored Ivy's great-grandmother's hope chest up here in the attic, which became Ivy's room a few months ago so the twins could have their own space. It sat at the end of her bed and smelled like cedar and old stuff. Inside, ancient pictures and clothes and knick-knacks were tucked away like secrets. There was even an old wedding dress in there, which Ivy thought was sort of creepy. When she asked about it, her mom told her that way back when, a hope chest was where a girl collected things she would need when she got married, *hoping* for the right boy to come along so her real life could start. Then her mother went on and on about how marriage had nothing to do with a girl's real life and how Ivy should hope for lots of different things, not just a boy, which was a relief.

She kept her real dreams in a notebook, where everything was a complete secret. Her hope chest was securely hidden away and guarded.

Ivy aimed the headlamp's beam at the purple-and-white cover of her notebook. It was one of those Decom-position notebooks, and she got it from her language arts teacher at school. She liked thinking about her notebook like that—*decomposition*. That's what it felt like to her, anyway: taking things apart in her head and putting them down on paper so she could figure out how they worked.

Outside, the thunder and lightning snapped right alongside each other, perfect secret drawing weather. Ivy flipped through the crinkly pages and caught a glimpse of a drawing she'd abandoned a few months ago as a hopeless case. She narrowed her eyes and glared at her family sitting on the grass in a large field. The grass in this field wasn't green, it was sil-ver and pink with a border of blue-leafed trees. There were Mom and Dad, their eyes shining and their mouths happy, holding Ivy's new twin brothers, Aaron and Evan, in their arms. Her sixteen-year-old sister, Layla, was right where she should be—sitting between their parents, grinning at Evan while Aaron wrapped his tiny hand around her finger.

Ivy scanned the page for inspiration. There was one person missing from this family portrait, and she couldn't figure out where to put her.

Where to put *Ivy*.

She glowered at the picture and flicked the page over so hard, it tore right out of the notebook. She nearly balled it up and tossed it toward her garbage can, which was already overflowing with other drawings gone awry. But it felt weird to throw away a picture of her family, even if she wasn't in it. Instead, she folded it up and stuffed it into her swirly blue pillowcase.

It wasn't the picture for a night like this anyway. This night needed one of her stormy pictures, like the one she was so close to showing Layla just a couple of weeks ago. The one she wouldn't ever, ever show her now.

She found the most recent drawing she'd been working on. There were dozens just like it in her notebook. Each one had some sort of house snuggled up in the branches of blue trees, trees on fire, trees made of gold, trees under the ocean, and trees at the tippy top of the highest mountain.

All of them had a girl with curly hair inside the house...and she wasn't alone. Another girl was in there with her. Sometimes they were standing, looking out at flame-colored hills in the distance. Sometimes they were lying down, tucked into sleeping bags that glowed because they were covered with tiny fireflies, like a hundred little night-lights. Sometimes they were reading or, like this one, facing each other and smiling.

Ivy didn't know who the girl was, but she wasn't Layla, and she wasn't her best friend, Taryn, or any of the other girls at school, who lately only wanted to talk about boys. Ivy was twelve years old and had never had a crush on a boy before, but maybe she just hadn't met one she liked. Or maybe she couldn't even get crushes.

That was her: Uncrushable Ivy.

But that didn't feel right either, so really, Ivy had no idea what she thought about crushes at all.

Which was exactly why the thunder outside was perfect for this picture. When Ivy looked at it, she felt a storm in her stomach. She felt a storm in her head. She felt a storm fizzing into her fingertips and toes.

Because in every single picture Ivy drew, she and that girl were holding hands. And they weren't holding hands like she and Layla used to hold hands when they ran down the street to play in the park. It wasn't the way she and Taryn used to hold hands when they ran through the sprinkler in Ivy's backyard, before Taryn got too cool to run through sprinklers and Ivy told her she was too cool for sprinklers too.

Ivy stared at the picture, chewing on her lower lip. Maybe she should rip them all out, starting with this one. She liked storms, but storms could be dangerous. And if Ivy had shown one of her stormy pictures to Layla, maybe her sister would've looked at her like she was weird.

She should definitely rip them all out.

Her hands shook as she closed her fingers around the top edge of the paper, ready to tear.

But she couldn't do it. Her hand wouldn't move that way. Instead, she swallowed the giant balloon in her throat and picked up her indigo-blue brush pen. While the real rain lashed at her window, she slipped some inky rain in between the drawn branches and leaves. She used her arctic-blue pen to zigzag in some lightning. She filled the sky with rolling silver clouds.

Before she could change her mind, Ivy colored in the girls. She used her lightest pink marker for her own hair, the color of sweet and fluffy cotton candy. In real life, Ivy's hair was strawberry blond, with frizzy curls her mother used to braid into smooth plaits. Lately, Mom never had time to do that, and Ivy certainly didn't want Layla to do it, so now her hair was a coiling mane of wildness all the time. But in Ivy's notebook, her hair was a soft and pretty pink, her curls always silky.

Ivy gave the other girl dark hair, the color of a raven's sleek feathers. She had dark eyes too—so dark blue they nearly matched the chaos of the sky. Both girls were happy inside that treehouse, their secret small and safe. Ivy wished she was there right now. It sounded like a wild adventure, sitting in that tree-house while the sky fell down around them.

Color filled up the page, and when Ivy was done, she sat back against her pillows. Her heart galloped in her chest, and she was out of breath like she'd just finished the mile run at school. It felt like the whole sky was inside her body, but she liked her picture.

She might have even loved it.

That was when she noticed how quiet it was outside.

Not the storm-was-over kind of quiet. A creepy kind of quiet. The kind of quiet that made all the tiny hairs on her arms stick straight up.

Then a few things happened at once.

One: The storm sirens in town went off, slicing through the quiet like an angry ghost.

Two: Ivy's bedroom door flew open, and her dad stumbled in, his eyes the size of dinner plates as the beam from her headlamp hit him in the face. She slapped her notebook shut.

"Ivy, let's go, honey." He held out his hand, and his voice was calm like it was when he told her she had to get three teeth pulled at the dentist last year. Which is to say, not very calm at all. Fake calm.

"What—"

"There's a tornado nearby, sweetie, no time to talk. We need to get to the storm cellar."

She kicked off her comforter and stuffed her notebook into her pillowcase, hugging it to her chest. She yanked off her headlamp just as Dad crossed the tiny room in two strides and grabbed her by the arm. Not hard enough to hurt, but hard enough to scare her. He pulled her toward the door just as the freakiest sound Ivy had ever heard loomed over the siren.

It sounded like a train. It grew louder and louder, a locomotive that couldn't possibly exist out here in her family's little part of rural Georgia.

Just as Ivy and her dad reached the top of the narrow attic stairs, a third thing happened.

Ivy's window exploded, spraying glass all over her bed and bringing the sky with it.

-‹‹‹◆›››-

CHAPTER TWO

Torn Away

Ivy's father never cursed, so when every bad word in the book flew out of his mouth, panic rose in Ivy's throat. She whimpered like a scared animal and nearly tripped over a pile of old clothes.

On her bed, her headlamp was still switched on, its light glinting off the glass scattered over her ruined sky-blue comforter. Her gauzy curtains were torn, wrapped around twigs and green-leafed branches. She got one last look at the mess before Dad yanked her in front of him and propelled her down the stairs to the second floor.

"Daniel!" Ivy's mother screamed her dad's name from the first floor. She sounded more scared than Ivy had ever heard her.

"Almost there, Elise!" Dad yelled.

Her dad was a big man, and he swooped Ivy into his arms, balancing her on his hip down the next flight of stairs.

Mom and Layla waited at the bottom of the staircase near the front door. Mom had Evan strapped to her chest in the baby carrier and Aaron wrapped in a soft yellow blanket in her arms. Layla gripped the baby bag, onesies and diapers overflowing. Everyone was breathing hard, and Aaron was wailing, his little three-month-old fingers grabbing at Mom's hair.

Pale pastels in blurry lines. That's how Ivy would draw all of them right now if she could.

The train outside got louder and louder.

Whoosh, whoosh, whoosh.

"Ivy," Mom gasped, reaching for Ivy with her free hand. Without a word, Layla stuffed red sneakers onto Ivy's feet.

"I can put on my own shoes," Ivy snapped.

"Not when Dad's carrying you, you can't," Layla said.

"All right, let's go," Dad said before Ivy could think of a good comeback. He nodded toward the door, and Layla threw it open.

Outside was a wild adventure, stuff full of wonder

and excitement when they were bright colors in a drawing, but not the kind Ivy had ever wanted to experience in real life.

The sound was painfully loud, that train huffing closer and closer. Underneath all that, there were *snap*s and *crack*s and *slam*s. The air felt muggier than their normal southern Aprils. It was a choking kind of feeling, like the earth couldn't breathe.

They spilled out the front door, Ivy's arms and legs still wrapped around her dad like a koala.

"Go, go, go," Dad said, nudging a frozen Layla with Ivy's foot.

"But we can't see anything!" Layla yelled over the wind. "What if it's out there?"

"The storm cellar is just around the corner of the house," Dad yelled back. "We'll run. It'll be okay."

"What if what's out there?" Ivy asked. She squinted through the dark, hoping for a train. A train would be so much better than what she knew was actually waiting for them.

"A tornado, Ives," Layla said, like she thought Ivy really didn't know.

"Elise, let Layla take—" Dad started, but Mom cut him off.

"I've got them. We need to go now."

Dad pressed his mouth flat, but nodded. His arms tightened around Ivy, his eyes never leaving Mom. "On three, girls. One...two...three!"

They leaped off the porch. The world flew around them like something out of *The Wizard of Oz*. Tree limbs blew through the air as if they were nothing but tissue paper, while bits of dirt and pebbles stung Ivy's face. Her hair floated upward as though she were underwater. Layla's old bike was in the grass near their gray minivan, the handlebars twisted the wrong way. Ivy saw their mailbox, *The Aberdeens* written in curvy script, dented and on its side near the big oak tree. The trunk of a pear tree was broken in two, its bottom half like bony fingers reaching for the sky. Ivy had no idea where the top half was. She didn't think she wanted to know.

Dad ran, one hand cradling Ivy's head. The rain soaked through Ivy's T-shirt and plaid pajama pants. She squeezed her eyes shut, hoping that when she opened them again, she'd be in her bed, drawing secret pictures that scared her. That kind of scary was a lot better than this kind.

"Daddy!" Layla screamed from behind them. Ivy's dad whirled around so fast, she saw spots.

"Oh no," he said. Ivy could barely hear him over the wind's fierce roar, and he set her on her feet. "Keep running for the cellar, Ivy."

"But—"

"Go!"

He took off back toward the house. Ivy saw Layla hovering over their mom, who was on her knees in the yard, screaming and trying to wrap Aaron back in her arms. He flailed on the grass, but his cries were swallowed up by the storm. After months of wishing he'd be quiet, Ivy would give anything to hear him screaming right now.

Dad scooped Aaron up while Layla helped Mom. She was gripping Evan's bald head and crying. Layla was crying and Dad was crying and Ivy was crying. The whole world was crying as everything fell apart.

Dad pushed Layla forward, and she fought the wind to get to Ivy while Mom and Dad struggled behind. Ivy couldn't see anyone clearly. They were covered in whirling hair and earth and sky. Ivy knew she should move, dive into the shelter that would tuck her underground, but she couldn't go in there alone.

"Ivy, go!" Layla yelled, her chestnut hair sticking to her face. Hail the size of golf balls fell from the sky, and Layla screamed, covering her head. When her sister reached her, Ivy wrapped her arms around Layla's waist, her pillow sopping wet and smooshed between them. They dragged themselves to the cellar, which was nothing more than a dirt room underground, built a century ago to store canned goods and potatoes. The entrance was a wooden door in the grass, and it shook and rattled against Ivy's palm as she wrapped her fingers around the handle.

Before she could get it open, a horrible screeching sound exploded behind them. Layla and Ivy turned in time to see their van lifted off the ground. It spun and the metal crumpled and then the whole thing disappeared into...nothing.

There was nothing there. Ivy scrunched up her eyes, trying to see, but when she did, she wished she hadn't.

Because there *was* something there. It was dark and huge and swirling, and it wanted to eat Ivy's whole world. If she drew it, she'd use nothing but dark charcoals and twisting lines that fell off the page.

"Inside, girls!" Dad yelled as he and Mom rushed up next to them.

Ivy yanked on the door, and it yawned open, revealing a little staircase descending into the dark. She went down first, but her ankle twisted on the last step, sending her sprawling over the dirt floor. Through the pillowcase, the corner of her notebook dug into her ribs.

"Move over, Ivy!" Layla screeched. Ivy scrambled up, her ankle screaming at her as she scurried into a corner so Mom and Dad could get into the cellar.

Dad set Aaron into Layla's arms before he ran back to shut the door. Ivy hugged her pillow to her chest, catching one more glimpse of that huge *nothing* looming up in front of her father. Then the door slammed shut and everything went dark.

-‹‹‹◆›››-

CHAPTER THREE

Undone

I vy used to think this cellar was magical. Back when Layla was a person she could trust, they'd open the cellar door and stretch out on the grass near the opening and make up stories about what was hiding down there in the dark. They weren't allowed to go in. Mom was worried that the door would close on them and get stuck and that no one would know where they were for hours and hours. Ivy remembered arguing with her, telling her that being trapped in a dark dungeon would be an adventure.

Well, it wasn't. It was damp and smelled like dirt and rotten potatoes, and Ivy's clothes were soaked, and she couldn't stop seeing that *nothing* swirling closer and closer. Who knew adventures could be so terrifying?

Above them, the door rattled and the sky roared. It wasn't a beautiful sound. It was ugly and had teeth behind it as the train chugged on and on. Ivy didn't know what it was running over and crashing into and ripping apart. She didn't want to know. She just wanted to go back to bed. She wanted her treehouse on top of a mountain.

Next to her, she thought Dad was holding Aaron again. She couldn't really see anything, but she heard him singing softly to keep her baby brother calm. Somewhere in the dark, Mom probably had her nose smooshed against Evan's head. Her headlamp, abandoned on her glass-covered bed, sure would have come in handy right now.

Layla fumbled for Ivy's hand. Ivy grabbed on, and she was so relieved that tears stung her eyes.

"Ivy," her sister said, squeezing her hand even tighter.

"Yeah?" Ivy's voice sounded tiny, and she could barely hear herself over the noise outside.

"Should we make this a Harriet story? Maybe it's not really a tornado. Maybe it's really the magical north wind come to transform us into..."

Layla's words trailed off like she was waiting for

Ivy to fill in the next line. They used to make up stories all the time. Mom had written and illustrated the Harriet Honeywell books, a chapter book series, for the past four years. She would always brainstorm with Ivy and Layla, letting them spill all their ideas into her lap. The first book was even dedicated to "My brilliant girls, without whom Harriet would never have been born." Stories, written and drawn, were in the Aberdeen girls' blood.

But Ivy didn't want to make up stories with Layla anymore.

"This isn't some fairy tale," Ivy said after a few seconds. "This is serious." She pulled her hand away from her sister's, thinking she'd feel triumphant and grown up. Really, Ivy just felt lost. She laced her own fingers together and squeezed, but it wasn't the same as Layla's hand in hers.

"I know it's serious, Ives." Layla sounded exasperated and hurt, and it made Ivy's stomach feel sour. She never talked to Layla like that. She knew she sounded like Mom when they used to get in trouble for playing hangman during church. Ivy didn't know how to be around her older sister anymore. Not since Layla and Gigi stopped being friends.

"This will be over soon," Dad said. "Then we'll go back to—"

But he never got to say whatever they might have gone back to because the loudest sound Ivy had ever heard exploded outside.

A *crunch* and a *smash* and a *crumble* and a *boom.*

Ivy clapped her hands over her ears and colored the sounds in her head. Carbon black and clear glass, the deep russet of their front porch. Squeezing her eyes closed, she shook her head, her hair tickling her arms. Those colors were scary, so she brushed them over with fuchsia starbursts and flowers with cobalt stems and a house nestled among gold-and-emerald-striped branches. She made a whole new and beautiful world, even as she worried that her own world was coming undone.

CHAPTER FOUR

Gone

It was over in a blink. All that noise turning into an eerie silence. Ivy's lungs seemed to have stopped working, and she knocked a fist against her chest to get them started again.

"Dad," Layla whispered. "What was all that?"

"I don't know," he said. His breathing must have just started up again too, because it sounded raspy and quick.

They sat for another few minutes, but it felt like five hours. Mom was totally silent, invisible in the dark. Ivy wanted to crawl into her lap, but her lap was pretty full with Ivy's baby brother right now, just like it always was.

"Is it over?" Ivy asked.

"I think so," Dad said. "Stay here. Let me check."

Ivy heard rustling as her dad stood up. Aaron squawked a little, and Layla shifted next to Ivy, so she knew her sister was holding him now. No one spoke, and Ivy was sure they all held their breath while the cellar door squeaked open. The storm siren got louder. It was barely any lighter outside, but Ivy made out Dad's silhouette against the greenish-black sky.

He climbed the steps, but stopped when his shoulders were out and pressed his fingers into the grass. His head turned this way and that. The storm siren wound down, like a balloon deflating on a slow leak. Ivy waited for a sigh of relief, a laugh, anything to tell them it was okay.

But none of that happened. In fact, a whole lot of nothing happened. Dad stood frozen on the third-to-top step, staring in the direction of their house.

"Dad?" Ivy asked. Mom shushed her. Dad stayed on the steps but tangled both his hands in his dark hair.

"Dad?" Layla asked. No one shushed her.

He didn't move, his hands still on top of his head.

"Daniel?"

Mom's voice seemed to snap him out of it. He released

a huge sigh and turned, his eyes roaming over Ivy and Layla until they landed on Mom.

Then he said a silly thing. A wild thing. An impossible thing.

"It's gone. Everything. It's all gone."

-‹‹‹◆›››-

CHAPTER FIVE

Rubble

Gone was not a word Ivy thought she would ever use to describe a house. A person, maybe. Summer vacation. The last of the chocolate cake. But not a house. And certainly not *her* house.

Dad was the funny one in their family, always trying to get her more serious mother to laugh. He called it his mission in life, to make his girls smile. So Ivy really hoped that was what he was doing when he said *gone*.

It's gone. Everything. It's all gone.

Possible translation: That rickety shutter on the living room window that always smacked against the house whenever the wind blew was gone. Then they'd all laugh over how Mom couldn't nag him anymore about replacing it.

But Ivy didn't think he was trying to be funny this time. He wasn't laughing. He wasn't grinning in that way that made the corners of his eyes wrinkle up.

Slowly, silently, her family climbed out of the cellar. Ivy was the last one. No one helped her, and her ankle ached, protesting her weight. She could already feel it swelling against the top of her shoe. She hugged her damp pillow and limped over to where her family stood, staring at the house.

Or at least, where the house used to be. Her dad was right. *Gone* was the perfect word to describe what Ivy was seeing right now.

Because there was nothing there. Nothing house-shaped, anyway. Just rubble. Just a mess. Just wood and that pink insulation stuff and tiles and clothes and food, all the colors of their world thrown together like a giant had had a temper tantrum. The stone porch steps were still there, right where they should be. So was the back wall of the sunroom, and part of a wall in the dining room with its rosebud wallpaper. Other than that, nothing. Even the brick chimney was crumbled, a pile of rust red and gray. Behind it, the sky was starting to lighten into a pale lavender, the clouds almost soft looking now. The whole storm was here and then gone.

24

Just like their house.

Ivy craned her head up, up, up to where her little attic room should be. There was nothing but a pinking sky. Some of the trees were cut in half, as though a huge pair of pliers had snipped off the tops. It was impossible to tell if any of the other houses around them had been hit too. The Aberdeen house sat on two acres of land. Their closest neighbor was Ms. Clement, a nice old lady with dyed red hair who always slipped Ivy a butterscotch candy whenever they ran into her in town, and she lived about a quarter mile away.

"Oh my God," Layla said, and Aaron squirmed against her chest. "Oh my God, oh my God."

"Okay, let's not panic," Dad said. That was his favorite phrase. *Let's not panic* when Mom's blood pressure got really high near the end of her pregnancy. *Let's not panic* when Aaron wouldn't stay asleep for more than thirty minutes at a time during the night. *Let's not panic* when Mom had to push back the next Harriet book deadline because she was so tired, she couldn't think straight.

"This is the perfect time to panic, Dad," Layla screeched. "We have no house. Where is our house?"

"Panicking won't make our house come back," Ivy

25

said, even though she kind of agreed with Layla. Panicking seemed like the perfect thing to do.

Layla glared at Ivy, but Dad just kept staring at the yawning pile of junk where their house once stood. Mom stared too, her mouth hanging open. Even like this, with her light red hair a mess and her nightgown all covered in dirt, she was pretty. Ivy felt a little twinge of longing for her mom to look at her and tell her it was okay, but she was quiet. Everyone was.

Ivy looked away, back into the sky.

"Did anyone grab their cell phone?" Dad asked.

No one answered. Ivy didn't even have a cell phone. Thirteen was when Layla got hers, Mom and Dad said, and thirteen was when Ivy would get one too. But now, no one had anything except Aaron and Evan's diaper bag.

"Is everyone all right?" Mom asked. "Layla?" She turned and ran her eyes over Layla's form.

"I mean, my body is fine, if that's what you're talking about," Layla said.

"Ivy?" Mom asked wearily.

Ivy thought of her ankle and nodded. It was no big deal. Not compared to their pile of a house.

Mom let out a breath before she started checking

the twins for marks or bruises, lifting their arms and inspecting their feet.

"Here's what we're going to do," Mom said when she seemed satisfied that no one was hurt. All their heads snapped toward her. She'd always been the captain of their ship. "We're going to go through the house...the mess...and see what we can find that we can use. Look for clothes and food, only what we actually need."

She looked around their yard and pointed to a pile of blue plastic near the oak tree that must have blown out of the old barn. Branches and leaves covered its surface. "Layla, go shake out that tarp, and we'll put everything we find over there."

"Hang on, I don't want the girls near the house," Dad said. "There might be some electrical issues. Maybe even a gas leak or something."

"Oh," Mom said, deflating. "I didn't think about that."

"We can still walk around the outside of the..." He frowned and his bottom lip actually wobbled as he waved toward the pile that used to be where they lived. His hand trembled. "See what we can find there."

"Okay." Mom rounded her shoulders back gently, trying not to wake Evan. Ivy couldn't believe he could sleep through all this. "Yes, let's do that."

"Why don't you go sit down with the boys, Elise," Dad said.

"I can help. I'll put Aaron on my back. Where's the other carrier—"

She clapped a hand over her mouth. Tears welled in her eyes, but she squeezed them away before they could slip down her cheeks. The other carrier, along with everything else they owned, was certainly nowhere to be found.

"This can't be happening," Mom whispered. "I can't believe this is happening."

Dad took Aaron from Layla and walked with Mom over to the tarp. He kept blinking and shaking his head, opening his mouth for words that never came. Ivy and Layla shook out the tarp, and then Mom sat down, her back against the oak tree. Ivy gave her the pillow to use however she needed, but she barely looked at Ivy, mumbling a thanks.

Instead of springing into action, they all sank down next to Mom. Ivy folded her legs and stared at her lap for a few seconds. She didn't want to look at their ruined house, but it was hard not to. It was like a wreck on the side of the road—it tugged at her eyes like a magnet.

She wasn't sure how long they stayed like that. She felt like crying, except that no one else was crying and she didn't want to cry alone. Plus, tears wouldn't help. They'd only make everyone feel worse, adding a whiny cherry to the top of this horrible sundae, so she stuffed her tears down, all the way down to her toes. It was easy, something she'd gotten used to doing in front of her family for the past year. It had been her job to keep Mom relaxed while she was pregnant, and worry-free after the twins were born.

Ivy stood up and limped over to the remains of their house. Her ankle throbbed, but she kept going. The air was damp and quiet and had a hint of that clean, green smell she used to love after spring rainstorms. Except now it was mixed with wood and metal and a sort of cloudy scent, like spring had caught a cold. Her eyes skittered through the mess for something familiar, any clue about where her room might have landed.

What a ridiculous idea—*where her room might have landed*. A hysterical laugh bubbled into Ivy's throat, but she forced it down. No one would understand why a laugh was the best thing right now. Much better than all this silence.

Finally, she saw something—the blue comforter

from her bed. Maybe her bedside table wasn't too far off.

"Ivy, what are you doing?" Layla called.

"Just looking," Ivy said, but she stepped on the rubble, right where it started arcing up into a little hill.

"Ivy, stop," Dad said, but Ivy took another step.

"Ivy Elizabeth!" Mom yelled.

"I just need to find something!" Ivy called back.

"Find what?" Layla said. "We need to find everything!"

Ivy moved forward a bit more, inching here and there to avoid the gaping holes between planks of wood and broken furniture. She tried not to think about how she was stepping all over their house. All over her entire life.

She set her bad ankle on the edge of what looked like the bathroom sink she and Layla shared. The chrome faucet was still flecked with dried toothpaste. Before she could go any farther, someone lifted her by her armpits.

"I told you to stop," Dad said, setting Ivy on her feet in front of the tarp. "It could be dangerous."

"I just needed my—"

"What, your stupid brush pens?" Layla said.

Ivy looked down, biting her lip so she didn't cry.

"Oh my God, that's it?" Layla asked. "You're worried about your pens right now?"

"Layla, easy," Mom said softly, but Ivy didn't think her sister heard.

"I mean, really, Ivy?" Layla said. "Look around you!"

Ivy didn't look around her. She didn't look at anything except her dirty red sneakers, her swelling ankle. She knew it was silly to worry about her pens right now, but she couldn't help it. They were nice pens, artist quality and fancy. You could refill the ink and replace the nibs, and they came with a blender pen. They cost a hundred and ten dollars for a pack of thirty-six colors. Ivy saved her allowance for seven months to buy them. Plus, they were *hers*. Her tools to create...well...her whole world.

This one certainly wasn't real anymore, if it ever was.

Ivy finally glanced up at her sister, but Layla was no longer looking at her. She was looking at the house, and tears were finally spilling out of her eyes. Ivy took a step forward because Layla was still her sister and sisters needed each other when things like this happened. But just when Ivy lifted her arms to hug her, Layla turned and collapsed next to Mom. She buried her face in Mom's lap, her shoulders shaking silently.

Mom had Aaron in her lap now too, but she managed to smooth her fingers through Layla's hair, murmuring to her softly.

Ivy stood and watched. And then she stood and *not* watched because looking at her family felt really lonely right now. Dad was next to her, but he was staring at the house, his hands on his hips. Every few breaths, he let out a gigantic sigh, over and over again.

Ivy thought about offering to go to Ms. Clement's house or maybe the Vance family on the other side of the woods, but she didn't want to go alone. She wasn't even sure she *could* go alone with her ankle hurting the way it was.

"What do we do now?" she asked, hoping her dad would know. He had to know. *Someone* had to know.

But he didn't answer, and when Ivy looked up at him, a few tears made their way down his dirt-streaked cheek.

-⫷⫸-

CHAPTER SIX

Rescued

The sun rose higher and higher, burning away the leftover clouds, and the sky went from lavender to too-bright blue.

"Dad?" Ivy slipped her hand into her father's. "Daddy?"

Finally, he blinked and took a shaky breath. He squeezed her hand once and then let her go, wiping his face on the crook of his arm.

"We need to call for some help," he said, turning back to Mom and Layla. "I'm going to head over to Ms. Clement's, make sure she's okay and see if we can use her phone."

"I'll come with you," Ivy said, desperate for something to do.

"No, sweetie, you stay here," he said.

"Please, I can help."

"Ivy, do what Dad says," Layla snapped.

Ivy scowled at Layla but didn't say anything. She turned away and sat under the oak tree.

Dad had just started jogging toward Ms. Clement's house when something rumbled from the driveway. Ivy looked up from where she was tearing leaves and gathering them into a little useless pile. Layla was still lying in their mother's lap, but she turned her head toward the noise.

Dad stopped and turned back, running toward the big silver truck bouncing up the gravel driveway. The driver was Xandra Somerset, a doctor who'd moved to Helenwood last summer. She was Mom's doctor, which meant she was a woman's doctor, but Ivy couldn't remember what that was called right now. Her daughter, June, who was Ivy's age, sat in the passenger seat, gaping at Ivy's nonhouse.

Another family—the Wayburns, who lived about two miles away and grew peaches—sat huddled in the bed of the truck. The youngest Wayburn, a toddler named Harris, wailed in his mother's lap.

Dr. Somerset stopped near the oak tree and parked the truck. She stared at the house for a bit too, then opened the door and got out.

Ivy stood up and limped closer.

"Hi, Daniel," Dr. Somerset said with a sigh. "Anyone hurt?"

He shook his head. "The Wayburns?" Dad asked, waving weakly at a shocked-looking Graham Wayburn.

"They're safe, but their house looks about like yours," Dr. Somerset said. Her eyes had dark circles under them, but Ivy remembered from the few checkups she went to with Mom that there was always a bit of a shadow there.

Dad swore softly, rubbing the back of his neck. "Do you know if Ms. Clement is okay?"

"She's fine. Missed her house completely, but it was bad, Daniel. The tornado went through downtown too."

"Is anyone seriously hurt?"

"No fatalities reported yet, but there are a lot of injuries. Some of them severe. June and I have been driving around trying to relieve the paramedics a bit and pick people up. Everyone who needs shelter is gathering at the elementary school."

"Right," Dad said, nodding at the ground. "Shelter. Okay." But he didn't move, just kept blinking at the wet grass.

"Do you have a car?" Dr. Somerset asked.

Dad frowned and looked around.

"The van's gone," Ivy said when he kept staring at the spot where their only car used to be. Right before Mom had the twins, their other car, an ancient CR-V, broke down, and Ivy's parents had decided it wasn't worth fixing. It was only about a twenty-minute walk into town, so they sold it to Trevor Kingston, who sold it for parts or something. Ivy thought they planned on getting Layla a car eventually, but *eventually* got swallowed up really fast by other stuff. And now this.

"Okay," Dr. Somerset said, nice and calm. "Are the twins all right?"

"I think so," Dad said. "Elise tripped on the way out of the house holding Aaron, but he was bundled up pretty tight. Could you check on him, though?"

"Of course." Dr. Somerset waved to June, who got out of the truck carrying a big gray messenger bag. She handed it to her mom and smiled at Ivy. It was a wobbly kind of smile, like she had no idea what to say, which was just fine with Ivy. She didn't know either.

Dr. Somerset walked over to Mom and squatted down. Layla finally sat up. "Have you nursed recently?"

Mom shook her head. "I need to."

Dr. Somerset dug a stethoscope out of her bag and checked both boys over. "They look just fine," she said, flipping the stethoscope behind her neck. "Let's get everyone into the truck."

Ivy breathed a sigh of relief as her family started moving. At least one thing was fine. Her ankle ached, but there was no way she was mentioning it with everything else going on. She could walk; that's all that mattered. She took her pillow from her mom and ran her hands over the hard outline of the notebook inside. Still safe.

"Wow," June said, standing next to Ivy. "This is awesome. I mean, just totally incredible."

Ivy turned toward her. "Excuse me?"

June waved her hand at the heap of a house, her mouth open and eyes wide. "Just look at it."

"Yeah, I can see it." Ivy's voice snapped and popped, but she didn't care. This was *awesome*? Was this girl serious? "So, me losing my house is . . . cool?"

June's dark eyes got even wider. "No! No, when I said *awesome*, I meant, like, inspiring great awe.

Daunting. Even fearsome. That a cloud of wind could do all that. It's terrifying and awful."

Ivy blinked at her. "Okay."

"I'm sorry," June said, looking down at her feet. "This always happens to me."

"What does?"

"My words. They sound right in my head, but when they come out of my mouth, it's not what I meant at all. My mom says I need to think before I speak." She glanced back at Dr. Somerset, and something sad flickered in her eyes, but Ivy was too distracted by the word *awesome* to care what June might be talking about.

"I'm sorry about your house," June said. "Really."

Ivy blinked at her some more.

June was in Ivy's homeroom at school. Her pixie-cut hair was dark and usually had a few little braids woven in somewhere. Ivy didn't know how she braided hair that short. June wore these cute dresses with leggings and talked a lot in class. Like, a lot. Sort of like the way she was babbling right now about *awesome* and *daunting*. And she always had the most bizarre lunches. Piles of vegetables and what looked like rice, but smaller. Ivy thought it was called keen-wa or something, and it was always in a giant glass container with one of those rubber lids. Not that veggies were an odd choice, but that's all June ever ate. Ivy had never seen her with a juice box or a cookie.

So basically, June Somerset was weird. Not that weird was bad. Weird was just weird. But Ivy was too scared about where her family was going to live—*how* they were going to live—to figure out anything else about June, so she just said "Thanks" and followed her family to the truck.

CHAPTER SEVEN

⫷⫷◆⫸⫸

Home for the Night

The truck bumped along the roads toward the elementary school, swerving around debris from the storm. As they headed into town, the houses got closer together, and the damage looked scarier. Huge tree branches lying on ripped-apart roofs, windows shattered, bikes and toys and trash scattered over lawns. A shredded tire lay in the middle of the road near Clayton Avenue.

Mom and Layla sat in the back seat, each holding a twin, so June was next to Ivy in the truck bed, every movement knocking their shoulders together. Ivy crushed her pillow against her chest, tracing her finger over one corner of her notebook. The Wayburns' youngest kid still hadn't stopped crying, but Ivy didn't mind. She was actually sort of jealous that he could cry like that and didn't have to worry about making things worse for everyone else.

"Are you okay?" June asked.

"I don't know," Ivy said.

June bunched her hands in the folds of her gray-and-white-striped tunic dress. "I just thought I should ask because you don't look okay, but when I think about it, asking whether or not you're okay seems really stupid right now. Of course you're not okay."

"No, I guess not."

"It's okay to not be okay. Most people don't think so, but I do. It has to be okay to not be okay all the time, don't you think?"

She was making Ivy dizzy.

"It was so fast," Ivy said, as her little farm disappeared behind a hill. "One minute, I was thinking about..." Ivy trailed off and gnawed on her lower lip.

"What?" June whispered, leaning closer to Ivy. She smelled like oranges and clean clothes. Ivy probably smelled like dirt and more dirt.

"Never mind," Ivy said, swallowing hard. Those few minutes before her dad busted into her room were like a dream, just like her picture of the two girls in the treehouse, holding hands, thinking they were safe and on some adventure—but it ended up being a disaster. Ivy hugged her pillow tighter and shook off the thought.

They pulled into Helenwood Elementary School's parking lot, already packed with cars. The building was made of red brick and two stories tall. Ivy had liked going to school there. It always seemed full of magic with its white columns on the front porch and tall flagpole. Now, though, it looked different. It was a *shelter*. Ivy was pretty sure she was going to hate this building forever from here on out.

They had to step around a lot of tree limbs on their way to the gym, but there didn't seem to be any more damage than that. The sky was still clearing, the clouds rolling back to reveal the blue underneath. Funny how that blue was always there, even when the rest of the earth was screaming and breaking into pieces.

"You're limping," June whispered to Ivy as they made their way up the sidewalk toward the gym's main doors.

Ivy shrugged and tried to even out her steps, but every time she pressed down on her foot too hard, tears bloomed in her eyes. She wiped them away and fell back behind her family so no one would see. Mom was already worried about the twins and the house, and Ivy didn't want Layla fussing over her. June slowed down to match Ivy's steps.

Inside, the gym was chaos. There were at least fifty people, and all of them were wearing dirty pajamas and had the same shocked expression on their faces as Ivy's dad. Families grouped together, claiming spaces on the shiny lacquered floor. People like June and her mom, people with clean clothes and neat hair, passed out blankets and pillows and what looked like the brown bag lunches Ivy got at school when she went on field trips.

Dr. Somerset led Ivy's family over to an empty space near the back wall and helped Mom sit down.

"You can get some clothes to change into over there," she said, pointing to the other side of the gym, where the clean people were handing stuff out. "There should be some things for the babies too. I need to check on a few other people, but I'll be back soon."

"Thank you, Dr. Somerset," Dad said. He scrubbed his hand over his stubbly chin. "I don't know how... I... Thank you."

Dr. Somerset smiled and squeezed his arm. "It'll be okay."

He nodded and took a deep breath like he really believed her. But Ivy knew better. *It'll be okay* was just something people said when they didn't know what else to say and things were really, really bad. It was exactly what Dad said before they ran for the storm cellar. But no one really knew what would be okay and what wouldn't.

Dad mumbled something about finding a phone to call the insurance company while Dr. Somerset started toward another family. June followed, calling out to her. Dr. Somerset stopped and pulled her daughter close, pressing the back of her hand to June's forehead. June shrugged her off and said something Ivy couldn't make out. Dr. Somerset looked up, her weary gaze landing on Ivy, a frown wrinkling her eyebrows.

They started walking toward Ivy.

Ivy backed up and turned around, placing her pillow next to Mom and kneeling to tickle Aaron's feet. He cooed at her, but it turned into a whine.

"I need to feed them," Mom said. She dug into the diaper bag and pulled out a burp cloth and a big sheet-like thing that looped around her neck that she used when nursing in public.

"Ivy?"

Ivy glanced over her shoulder and saw Dr. Somerset.

"Are you hurt?" she asked.

"No. No, I'm fine—"

"She's limping," June said. Ivy glared at her.

"What?" Mom said, her eyes finding Ivy. She picked up Evan and dipped him under the nursing sheet, cradling him against her chest. "Honey, what happened?"

"Nothing. I twisted my ankle a little in the cellar. It's not a big deal."

"Why didn't you say anything?" Mom asked. "Layla, you didn't see this?"

Layla, who had picked up Aaron, tilted her head at her sister. Ivy looked away. For the past year, Layla was usually the one Ivy went to when she had a headache or cut her toe while playing outside barefoot because she hated putting on shoes. Part of her don't-stress-Mom-out plan of action. About a week after Aaron and Evan came home from the hospital, Ivy started her period for the first time. Mom had turned into Zombie-Mom, so Layla got Ivy pads and stood outside the bathroom door, talking her through the whole thing.

"I don't know," Layla said, kissing Aaron's cheek. "I guess Ivy's old enough to look after herself."

There was a tinge of hurt in her voice, but Ivy ignored it. She waited for Mom to disagree with Layla, to say that Ivy wasn't *that* old, because if twelve wasn't old enough to stay up past nine thirty on a school night, then it certainly wasn't old enough to fend for herself in a tornado.

But Mom didn't say anything like that. She sighed and peeked at Evan through the neck of the nursing sheet.

"Layla," she said, "why don't you go find us some more blankets and clothes. I'd rather not lay the boys on this dirty floor. And maybe a few granola bars or something."

"Yeah, okay." Layla glanced at Ivy's ankle one more time before walking away with Aaron.

"Let me take a look," Dr. Somerset said. She motioned for Ivy to sit down and Ivy did, her throat suddenly all thick and annoying. Dr. Somerset untied Ivy's sneaker, but didn't take it off. She poked at Ivy's ankle and moved her foot around until Ivy sucked in a sharp breath.

"That hurt?" Dr. Somerset asked.

"A little."

"Nothing's broken," she said. "It's probably just a

46

sprain. I'm going to wrap it, but leave your shoe on, okay? If you take it off right now, you might not be able to get it back on until the swelling goes down. We'll find some ice for it. June, could you?"

"Yes, I can do that!" June said, weirdly excited, and took off in search of ice.

Dr. Somerset started wrapping Ivy's ankle in a beige bandage. She was quick and efficient and didn't say another word. She was like a rock, while June was all water.

Five minutes later, she finished and left, promising to check back later. Mom rubbed Ivy's back, but her touch was uneven because she kept moving around and adjusting Evan while she nursed. Eventually, Ivy scooted away a little so her mom didn't feel like she had to comfort her. Mom didn't even notice. She didn't notice a lot lately.

It could be because Ivy's ankle hurt, but her chest felt tight, just like it did when she first found out that Mom was pregnant with the twins. She'd been excited at first. Twins! Brothers! Or another sister, maybe two! But then Dad got right down to business, talking about how they all had to play their part and pitch in. Mom was forty-one years old, so the pregnancy was what they called "high risk." Stress was dangerous. So was exhaustion and heavy lifting. Mom had to stay in bed for the last two months of the pregnancy.

Ivy was happy to help, but it was hard. She was worried about Mom a lot, and the twins ended up coming early anyway. Since then, she felt like she'd barely seen her mother. It was all twins all the time with Ivy's family.

When she looked up from her ankle, she saw June jogging back across the gym, bringing Taryn, Ivy's best friend, with her.

"Ivy!" Taryn yelled from ten feet away. She ran over and collapsed next to Ivy. Ivy got a whiff of her peony body lotion, and it smelled so familiar and nice after the smell of dirt and sweat stuck up her nose for the last few hours.

"Is your house really gone?" Taryn asked.

There was that word again—*gone*. Ivy had no clue what she was supposed to say.

Yep! Sure is! Totally vanished!

Any response felt weird and didn't match up with what was actually happening, so Ivy nodded.

"Wow," Taryn said.

"Yeah."

"I'm so sorry."

"It's okay."

June frowned at Ivy and handed her a plastic bag full of ice. Ivy took it and pressed it to her ankle, avoiding June's eyes.

"Annie Demetrios's house flooded, but it's still in one piece," Taryn said, craning her neck to look around the gym. Taryn waved at Annie a few families down. She waved back, but didn't smile as she sipped from a foam cup.

"Drew is here too," Taryn went on. "His house wasn't wiped out, but they can't stay in it right now. The roof is messed up. And they think he broke his arm."

"Oh no, really? Is he okay?" Ivy asked. Drew played soccer for their seventh-grade team. It was a fall sport, so they were done, but Ivy was pretty sure he played with a local league in the spring.

Taryn shrugged and knotted her fingers together. She'd had a crush on Drew Dunaway ever since Ivy and Taryn figured out what crushes were. They sat with him and his friends at lunch sometimes. All he and Taryn ever talked about was soccer and superhero movies. There was nothing wrong with soccer

49

and superhero movies, but Ivy didn't have much to say about them, which left her chewing her turkey sandwiches or doodling on everyone's napkins in silence whenever they sat with him.

"You can go hang out with Drew if you want," Ivy said.

"I said hey to him. He seemed pretty out of it. I think he's on some painkillers, and they're making him loopy," Taryn said, pushing her dark blond hair over her shoulder. Her straight bangs cut a perfect line across her forehead. Ivy wished she could get away with bangs.

"Besides," Taryn said, "I need to stay with you. That's why I came by." She snuggled into Ivy's side, and Ivy couldn't help but smile.

Taryn and Ivy had been best friends since the summer before kindergarten, when they met during swimming lessons at the rec center. Taryn flounced over in her bright yellow bathing suit to where Ivy's mom was trying to fit a pair of goggles over Ivy's head of thick hair. Taryn told her she wanted to swim the butterfly. Ivy thought that sounded magical—*swimming the butterfly*—like something out of a fairy tale. It wasn't until years later that Ivy realized Taryn's dad had been a swimmer in college and had taught her the names of all the swimming strokes. That was decidedly less fantastical, but by then, Ivy was hooked on Taryn's bubbly laugh and the way she wrinkled her nose at anyone who made fun of Ivy's poofy hair and freckles.

"So what are you going to do?" Taryn asked now, waving at Ivy's mom, who barely managed a weary smile. Of course Taryn would ask this. She was all action. She was a windup toy zooming over a hardwood floor.

"I don't know," Ivy said.

"Where are you going to live?"

"I don't know."

"Are you still going to be able to do soccer camp with me this summer?"

"I—" *I hope not* nearly fell out of Ivy's mouth. Just last week, she'd agreed to go with Taryn to the camp, and really, soccer was fine. It was almost, kind of, sort of, what Ivy would call fun. And she didn't suck at it. But to do the camp, she had to miss this young artists' workshop her art teacher had told her about at Thoman-Brown College in town, which was definitely, absolutely something Ivy would call fun. But it was fine. The soccer camp was for girls thirteen and under only, which meant Taryn and Ivy could do it together, away from stupid sisters and the doe-eyed look Taryn got every time she saw Drew.

"I don't know," Ivy finally said after a deep breath.

"But what about—"

"I don't think she knows anything right now." June's voice was soft and even, but firm. She sat down on Ivy's other side and adjusted the ice pack on her ankle, which had slipped and was sweating all over the floor.

Taryn's cheeks turned pink, and she fiddled with the strap of her red tank top. She glanced at Ivy, like she was waiting for her to give a different answer, but Ivy certainly didn't have one.

"Right," Taryn said softly. "Sorry. Duh."

"It's all right," Ivy said, though nothing felt all right.

"I'm sure it'll all work out," Taryn said. Then her blue eyes widened, and she clapped her hands together. "Maybe you could live with me for a while!"

Taryn's mom was an interior decorator. Their house was very big and very stylish, full of squashy couches and beautiful throw pillows, silk curtains lining every window.

"I don't think your mom wants my whole messy family in her house," Ivy said.

Taryn laughed. "Oh gosh, no. I just meant you."

"Oh." Ivy looked over to where Mom had Evan propped on her shoulder. She patted his back, her head leaning against his smaller one, her eyes closed. For the past few months, Ivy had daydreamed once or twice—okay, maybe three times—of getting away from her family. Just up and running away. Would they notice? Would they even care?

"I'll have my mom talk to yours," Taryn said. "It might help things."

"Help what?"

Taryn shrugged. "Just...things. Your parents have a lot going on with the twins and now this. I mean, wow, right? It might be easier if they didn't have to worry about you for a while."

Ivy blinked at her. "Right. Easier." She tried to swallow the huge knot in her throat, but it just kept getting bigger and bigger, a balloon swelling on a helium tank. It was one thing for Ivy to wonder about being without her family. It was another thing for Taryn to say out loud that Ivy's absence would probably be a good thing.

"Oh, maybe I should read your cards!" Taryn said. She dived into her big bag and pulled out her beloved tarot deck. When they were in fifth grade, Taryn got really into tarot cards. Even though she didn't know how to read them, Taryn loved to shuffle, shuffle,

shuffle and then make Ivy draw one, proclaiming whatever card Ivy held in her hand was her destiny.

Ivy was pretty sure tarot didn't work like that.

June cleared her throat. "So, Taryn, are you going to ask Drew to the Spring Dance?"

Taryn squealed a little and kept shuffling. She launched into all the reasons why she should ask Drew and all the reasons why she shouldn't, all of which Ivy had heard before. She never dealt the tarot cards, just kept on shuffling, Ivy's fresh tragedy forgotten for a while. Ivy used the time to get her breath back.

June nodded along with her, excited about everything Taryn was saying, although Ivy had no idea how June even knew that Taryn liked Drew. June was funny like that, talkative and loud in class, but at lunch and during gym, she got quiet. She ate her weird lunch at the other end of the long rectangular table where Taryn and Ivy sat, and she just...watched. Not in a creepy way. Just like she was taking everything in. Ivy had never seen her hang out with anyone in particular. Not really.

Right now, Ivy felt June glance at her a few times while she listened to Taryn. When Ivy finally met her eyes, June gave her a small smile. Ivy gave her a grateful smile back.

-‹‹‹◆›››-

CHAPTER EIGHT

Sisters

Taryn didn't stay long. Before she left, she told Ivy, "It'll all be okay," but Ivy nearly growled at her. Ivy didn't want to hear that right now because when anyone said it, she had to smile and nod and pretend like what they were saying was true. She felt a weird sort of relief when Taryn bounced away with a promise to ask her mom about Ivy staying with them.

June's mom called her away too, and after a few hours of doing nothing—Ivy stared at all the dirt-colored water spots on the gym ceiling for she didn't know how long—the room eventually quieted down.

Dad came back with a million numbers scribbled all over a pad of paper. He and Mom sat for a long time, whispering with their heads bent together so Ivy and

Layla couldn't hear. The twins were asleep in a nest of borrowed blankets next to Mom. Once or twice, Ivy saw her father wipe at his eyes and Mom lean her forehead against his. The whole thing made Ivy squirm. She'd seen her dad cry before, but at sappy stuff, like when Layla won MVP for her lacrosse team last year or when he held Aaron and Evan for the first time in the hospital room. Ivy had never seen him sad-cry until today. But his great-grandparents had built their house. He'd been born there. Of course he was going to sad-cry.

The sun started to set, its rays beaming through the high windows in the gym, turning the wheat-colored floor into a deep gold. Ivy and her family ate peanut butter and jelly sandwiches out of brown paper bags. Again. It tasted like school. Pretty soon after that, everyone started falling asleep under scratchy blankets and musty-smelling pillows.

Ivy lay down, arranging her own pillow under her head so that her notebook was against the floor and turning this way and that to get comfortable. Her eyelids felt heavy, like someone was yanking on them, but she couldn't sleep. The gym smelled like rain and stale bread and what she imagined a boys' locker room might smell like. Every few seconds, someone coughed or whispered or flicked on a flashlight. Ivy couldn't stop fidgeting, her legs all jumpy and her fingers twitchy. She sat up and looked around the dim room at the red glow from the EXIT signs and the lumpy shapes sprawled all over the floor.

And it hit her. *Pow. Boom. Crack.*

She was homeless.

She didn't have a home anymore.

She didn't have her bed or that silly-looking head-lamp her dad had bought for her when they went camping or any of her clothes or her little attic room where she could stay up late and draw pictures that she loved with her stupid brush pens.

She didn't even have brush pens.

Sobs crawled up her throat, and she finally let them out. Turning on her side, she curled into a ball and buried her face in her pillow, soaking the cotton. When she felt nice and empty, she opened her eyes and saw Layla a few feet away from her.

She was doing the exact same thing as Ivy.

Her back was to Ivy, but she was tucked into herself and her shoulders were shaking. Every now and then, she lifted her hand and swiped at her eyes. Ivy wanted to get up and go to her. She wanted to snuggle into her sister's side, let Layla smooth her tangly hair, and ask her to tell a story. Ask her to let Ivy tell one too.

But she couldn't, not since the conversation she overheard between Layla and her best friend, Gigi, two weeks ago. Now Ivy wasn't sure who Layla was anymore.

Ivy wasn't sure who Ivy was either.

And she definitely wasn't sure about what her sister would think if Layla really knew all Ivy's secrets.

One thing Ivy was sure about—she was way too scared to find out.

That night two weeks ago, Gigi was in Layla's room. At least three times a week, Gigi ate dinner at the Aberdeen house. Her mom was a nurse and worked nights, and even after the twins were born and they ate frozen casseroles brought by neighbors and church members for weeks on end, Gigi still came over to eat with them.

Ivy loved Gigi. She was tall and curvy and had hair that looked like fresh honey and always, always, always had her nails painted some wild color. Neon yellow. Electric blue. Aubergine purple. She reminded Ivy of an elf. Gigi and Layla had been best friends since preschool, and Gigi was great about including Ivy. Ivy totally got how rare that was, for a teenager to be cool with a kid bursting into her best friend's room and bouncing on the bed, begging them to straighten her hair or paint her nails or just let her listen to the latest high school gossip. But that was Gigi, even when Layla tried to kick Ivy out.

Taryn loved Gigi too, and during the summer, the four of them would go to the rec center pool and lie in the sun and cannonball into the water. It always felt like they were actually friends instead of two kids Ivy's mom had begged Layla and Gigi to take with them.

That night, Ivy had just finished a bit more detail on a stormy treehouse drawing. Their house was total chaos, babies screaming all the time, diapers everywhere, dirty burp cloths thrown over the backs of couches and chairs. Ivy didn't even know Gigi had come over. She just knew that she was ready to show Layla her drawing, because every time she worked on it, she ended up crying or her chest would tighten and she couldn't get enough breath. She felt like she was going to explode, and she knew she couldn't talk to her mom right now, but she had to talk to someone.

Layla was almost as exhausted as their parents,

helping out in the middle of the night when the twins woke up for feedings. But she and Ivy had gotten even closer lately, bonding while the family changed into something new and also kind of scary. Layla seemed to know when Ivy was feeling left out or invisible, and she always made her feel better, whether it was just inviting Ivy into her room to listen to music or making her famous hot chocolate with steamed half-and-half, one giant marshmallow floating in the middle. Yes, it was time to tell Layla. Ivy *wanted* to tell Layla and only Layla.

Ivy descended from the attic and walked down the old wood floors to Layla's room. Her door was open a crack, and Ivy was just about to knock when she heard Gigi's voice, which sounded weirdly watery and clogged.

"...not sorry I didn't tell you. I wasn't ready. You have to understand that."

"I'm trying to, but..." Layla sniffed, and her voice broke a little as though she was trying to talk through tears. Everything in Ivy locked up, and her heart felt like a brassy gong in her chest.

"But I guess I really don't get it," Layla went on. "This is me. I'm your best friend, and I had to hear it from Jesse Ryder, who said he saw you two kissing in your car. How do you think that made me feel?"

"Lay, this isn't about you."

"I'm not saying that it is. But you have a girlfriend, Gigi. A *girlfriend*."

Ivy's notebook almost slipped out of her fingers. She gripped it tighter at the last minute, but she was almost positive Layla and Gigi heard the crinkling of the paper. For a few seconds, no one said anything. Ivy couldn't even breathe. That word—*girlfriend*—kept exploding in her head like fireworks.

"I don't know what to think about this, Geej," Layla said. "I can't process this. I can't—"

Gigi made a frustrated sound. "By all means, ignore what I'm saying and make this about you. Again. How do you think I feel? I didn't want you to find out like that. I've wanted to talk to you about it for years. *Years*, Lay. But I was still figuring it out. I haven't even told my parents. Bryn's only told her mom. Her dad is still clueless."

Ivy didn't exactly understand everything they were saying, but the gist was pretty clear.

Gigi liked girls.

Gigi had a girlfriend.

And Layla hadn't known until today.

Ivy waited for Layla to tell Gigi that it was okay. That she got it. That she loved Gigi just the way she was.

But that didn't happen. Instead, they sat there for a while, their sniffling the only sound. Finally, Ivy heard the bed creak as someone stood up.

"I guess I'll see you at school," Gigi said softly.

The door swung open, and Ivy backed into the bathroom's dark doorway across the hall. The tile seeped cold through her socks, and it smelled like Layla's ginger perfume and toothpaste. Gigi came out of the bedroom and wiped her eyes with both hands. She stood there for a minute, breathing in and out, in and out.

And then she left, and that was the last time Ivy saw her.

-≪≪◆≫≫-

CHAPTER NINE

Letters to the World

I vy waited until Layla's shoulders were moving up and down with slow, even breaths. Then she kicked off the blanket that smelled like hot dogs and stood up. Ivy patted her pillow, feeling the edges of her notebook, and then pulled the blanket over it and bunched up the edges. It definitely didn't look like a person was sleeping under there, but it would have to do.

Tomorrow was Tuesday and school had been canceled, but the principal had announced that they wanted everyone to stick to the bathrooms and the gym. But right now, Ivy was a homeless girl who didn't care.

After she limped-tiptoed down the main hallway, she pushed open the double doors into the library. Ivy slipped inside and pressed her back against the door while gulping deep breaths. Then she gulped a bit more because she felt like she hadn't breathed enough since the storm hit. This was the closest thing to her little attic room that she was going to get right now.

After her lungs felt good and full, she wandered up and down the shelf-lined aisles. Moonlight streamed through the windows, making the whole room look silvery. It was eerie and beautiful and quiet. Posters quoting Shakespeare and *Alice's Adventures in Wonderland* and *Oliver Twist* hung on the walls. Right above the little poetry section, there was a poster of a girl named Emily Dickinson in an old-fashioned dress with her hair coiled in a bun. Her poems were weird, all dashes and confusing words. Ivy read a few in her language arts class a few months ago during a poetry unit. Her teacher said that Emily hadn't gone out in public a lot and that her poems were never read when she was alive. She hid them away, but now she was famous.

This is my letter to the world,
that never wrote to me...

That was what the poster said, in a handwriting font, as if Emily herself scribbled it one night by candlelight.

Maybe on a night when she was feeling really lonely and just needed to get things out of her head, even though no one was listening. Ivy stared at the words now, and her throat ached. She wished she had brought her notebook to write it down. Instead, she repeated the words, over and over, until she was sure she memorized them.

"What do you think that means?" a voice whispered.

It startled Ivy enough that she yelped and swung around.

"Oops, sorry," the voice said. "I didn't mean to scare you."

Ivy didn't answer, her heart still halfway up her throat. Whoever was talking to her stood, but the light from a cell phone shined in Ivy's eyes, and she couldn't see anything except a blocky silhouette.

"Could you maybe..." Ivy squinted and shaded her eyes with her hands.

"Oh yeah, sorry."

The light lowered and there was June Somerset, books puddled around her feet.

"What are you doing here?" Ivy asked.

"What are *you* doing here?" June asked.

"I'm...I'm..."

"Yeah. Me too."

Ivy frowned. "It looks like you're reading. I wasn't reading."

"You were reading that poster."

Ivy sighed. This girl was exhausting. "But why are you here? At the school, I mean. Isn't your house okay?"

"Yeah, but my mom wanted to stay the night in case someone needed her. Mrs. Lewis's house got messed up, and she's, like, six months pregnant or something. Pepper Hillson is diabetic, and they had to find some insulin for her. Then there's your mom and the twins."

"Right. The twins." Ivy twisted her fingers into the hem of her borrowed shirt. Layla had grabbed it for her. It was about two sizes too big and smelled like sweaty socks. "Isn't your dad at home?"

June went very still, toeing the edge of one of the books. "My dad lives in California."

"Oh. Sorry. I didn't know."

June shrugged and then nodded her chin toward the Emily Dickinson poster. "So, what do you think that means?"

Ivy turned and looked at the quote. She scrunched up her face as she read it again, not that she needed to. The words were printed on her brain like ink on paper.

"Um...maybe..." Ivy stumbled over her words. She didn't want June to think she didn't know, but now that she thought about it, she wasn't exactly sure what the quote meant. There was just something about it that she liked.

"Yeah," June said, like Ivy had said something profound. "What was her letter to the world? And why would the whole world write *her* a letter anyway?"

Ivy shrugged, but kept looking at the poster. She felt like she knew the answer, but it was hiding, like a secret she was afraid to tell.

June plopped back onto the floor and shined her phone's light on the pile of books. "Want to join me? I'm reading some old favorites."

"Sure, I guess." Ivy sat down across from June. The carpet was so thin that Ivy could feel the cold from the concrete underneath. As June's light swept across one of the titles—*Harriet Honeywell and the Mermaids of Hurricane Cove*—Ivy sucked in a breath.

"I love these books," June said, picking up a thin paperback and opening to the first page. "Have you read them?"

Ivy swallowed. "Um. Yeah."

"I know they're for younger kids, but they make me so happy. I've read all four about a million times. I really love the drawings, you know? Harriet is so funny, but Greenleigh is my favorite."

Ivy couldn't help but smile at that. In the first book,

when Harriet accidentally set sail in her uncle's boat and mermaids came to help her get back to shore, it was Ivy's idea to create Greenleigh. Greenleigh was a mermaid who became Harriet's best friend for the rest of the series. Ivy even got to name her, and she'd helped Mom on every single Harriet book since.

But Mom hadn't had time to talk about Harriet at all lately.

Ivy got up and limped toward the checkout counter, where she found a piece of plain white paper in the printer. Then she borrowed a nicely sharpened pencil from the blue mason jar on the librarian's desk. She hobbled back to June, stretched out on her stomach, and started to draw.

Except for the low *tick* of the wall clock and June's soft breathing, the room was quiet. Ivy didn't need to look at the book as she drew. She knew this character by heart. She had created this character, in a way. It didn't look exactly like her mom's drawing, but it was close enough. Plus, Ivy liked that it wasn't an exact copy, that it was hers. As she shaded in Greenleigh's short hair, she realized the mermaid looked a little like June. After that, she erased the nose and turned it up a bit more, made the eyes a little rounder, the top lip a bit thinner. Soon, it *was* June. Or a mermaid version of June, anyway. But with her diamond-patterned mermaid tail, frayed tank top, and the little beaded seashell necklace around her neck, the drawing was also Greenleigh. It was a perfect blend.

When she was finished, Ivy handed the drawing to a wide-eyed June.

"Wow," June breathed, holding the paper like it was made of the thinnest glass. "You're really good."

"Thanks."

"I'm not really good at anything." June blinked at the drawing and ran her finger over Greenleigh-June's pixie hair.

"Everyone's good at something," Ivy said.

"Not me. I never really—" June's face sort of crumpled, but she smoothed it out really quickly. She shook her head. A smile landed on her face and stayed put. "Maybe you could teach me!"

"Teach you...what?" Ivy asked.

"How to draw, silly." June waved the paper at Ivy. "You're good enough."

"Oh. Well. I don't think...I mean, drawing is just something I do. I never learned."

"I know I'll never be as good as you, but I could learn some basics, right? Like, I can't even draw a decent cat. Stick figures all the way for me."

Ivy thought about how she first started drawing, how the shapes and shades sort of fell out of her. Still, her mom had taught her some techniques, and they helped. Ivy got better. Plus, a minute ago, June had looked so sad that she wasn't good at anything, and now she looked so excited about drawing that Ivy couldn't say no.

"I guess we could try it," Ivy said.

June squealed and clapped, then smacked her hand over her mouth. She was so cute that Ivy couldn't help but laugh.

"Oh, but instead of a cat, let's do a whale!" June said.

"A whale?"

"A blue whale."

"I don't have any colored pencils."

June laughed. "No, an actual blue whale, the largest mammal on the planet." June grabbed her phone and tapped the screen a couple of times before holding it out to Ivy. There, a huge whale swam through deep blue water.

"Used to be," June said, setting her phone back down, "scientists thought the aorta in their heart was big enough for a human to swim through. Now we know it's not, and their whole heart is about the size of a golf cart. I still love the idea, though."

"Love...what idea?"

Even in the dim light, June's eyes sparkled. "That a heart could exist that's big enough to fit a whole person inside. Isn't that cool?"

A smile pulled at Ivy's mouth. "You know a lot about whales."

"Well, I've had a *lot* of time to think about them. And dolphins too. And photography and poetry and archeology and parallel dimensions and all sorts of stuff."

Ivy blinked.

"Oh," June said, pressing her hands to her face. "I made it awkward, didn't I? I'm always doing that. I'm sorry."

"Don't be sorry," Ivy said. Suddenly she wanted to put June at ease. She wanted June to smile. "It's not awkward, it's...interesting."

Then June did smile. "Yeah?"

"Yeah. Now let's draw a whale."

"A *blue* whale."

Ivy laughed. "The bluest of blue whales."

After they got some more paper and borrowed another pencil, they stretched out on their stomachs, hip to hip, and June Somerset learned how to draw a blue whale.

CHAPTER TEN

Lost

Ivy and June whispered and giggled all the way back to the gym, papers crinkling between them.

"I'm going to name her Emily," June said, beaming down at her freshly drawn blue whale.

"Why Emily?"

"For Emily Dickinson. Maybe this blue whale is my letter to the world."

June grinned and Ivy laughed. She'd laughed more in the past hour than she had in weeks. Maybe months. They'd drawn for hours, and June was hilarious as she learned, pressing her tongue to her top lip in concentration and scrunching a hand into her hair when she got frustrated. Still, she smiled through the whole process, like drawing a simple whale was the best thing that ever happened to her. She wanted to learn how to draw people next, and Ivy agreed to teach her.

Now, as June practically glowed next to her, Ivy's stomach fluttered with happiness. She tried to remember a time when she and Taryn had so much fun that it made her all giddy and trembly.

She couldn't.

If she drew this feeling, it would be softly flowing waves the color of a delicate pink ballet slipper. In fact, that's exactly what she planned to do—draw this feeling in her notebook, maybe a few sketches of June learning to draw. Ivy never thought she could do something that could make someone so happy.

They stepped inside the gym, where everyone was just starting to wake. The lights were still off, but the morning sun turned the room a pinkish gold. Ivy tried to breathe it in, like the color could untie the sudden knot in her throat. People were everywhere. Yawning, coughing, stretching. Most were folding up their blankets and tossing them into piles in the corners of the room, but some just lay awake on the floor or propped against the concrete walls, staring into space. Ivy could hear Aaron crying.

Ivy would rather go back to the library and teach

June how to draw another whale. Or maybe a dolphin this time.

"Uh-oh," June said. She wasn't looking at Ivy, so Ivy followed her gaze across the room to where June's mother was glaring at her, hands on her hips.

"I've got to go," June said. Before Ivy could even get out an "Okay, see you," June jogged over and joined her mother, whose mouth immediately started moving. Ivy couldn't hear her, but she could tell Dr. Somerset was mad. Her hands fluttered in the air as she talked before she rested them on June's shoulders. June shoved them off, and her fingers balled into fists. She stalked away and smacked the back exit doors open. Sunlight poured into the room before swallowing June whole.

Ivy wanted to go after her and apologize for getting her into trouble, but Layla called her name and waved her over.

"We're going to a hotel," Layla said. Her sister looked so tiny in her clothes, an Auburn Tigers sweatshirt and too-big sweatpants from the donation pile. Ivy's own secondhand clothes felt sticky from her being awake all night.

"What? Why?" Ivy asked.

"Where else are we going to go, Ivy? Move in with Grammy?"

"I thought we might go..." But Ivy had no idea where they might go, probably because she hadn't thought about it at all. Her grandma lived in Florida, in one of those assisted-living places that always smelled like baked chicken. No way she wanted to go there, but she couldn't go home either. She didn't have a home. It was a gut punch every time she thought about it.

Layla handed her a cereal bar—blueberry, gross— and then started pulling on her boots. Ivy blinked at the blue-foiled wrapper.

"Did you sleep okay, Ivy?" her mother asked. She sat against the wall, working Evan's arm through a onesie. Both boys were lying on a blanket in their diapers, but Ivy knew it was Evan because his head was totally bald. Aaron had a head full of Dad's dark hair.

"Slept great," Ivy said flatly. Her mother hadn't even noticed Ivy wasn't next to her all night.

"Did you find enough clothes to last you a while?" Layla asked as she finished lacing her boot.

"Not really. I just have whatever you brought me yesterday."

Layla picked up Aaron and then laid him back down

so he was facing her. She pulled a clean onesie from the diaper bag. "Do you want me to come with you to get more?" she asked. "I can help you find something cute."

"I can find it myself."

Layla sighed. "Maybe you should call Taryn. She and her mom just brought by a bunch of doughnuts for everyone, so she might not be home yet, but I'm sure someone has a phone you could use. Maybe Taryn can help you feel better."

"Well, maybe you should call Gigi."

Ivy would like to be able to say that Gigi's name came out of her mouth because she was so used to Gigi being a part of their lives, but that would be a lie. She watched Layla, waiting to see how she would react.

But Layla didn't say anything. She blinked at Ivy a few times before turning away, kissing Aaron on the cheek.

Ivy stomped off toward the donated-clothes pile, shame and anger and sadness a giant knot in her chest. She caught a glimpse of June, who had come back inside and was now collecting blankets in one pile and pillows in another.

Pillows.

Ivy went back to her family's little campsite and

looked around for her pillow, but there were only a couple of cereal bar wrappers and some bottles of water. All the blankets they used last night were gone.

"Where's my pillow?" Ivy asked. She tried to keep the screech out of her voice, but she was pretty sure she failed.

Layla shook a raggedy teddy bear with a rattle in its stomach at Aaron and glanced up at her. "What pillow?"

"*My* pillow. The blue one. The only thing I brought out of the house."

Layla looked around as Aaron grabbed a chunk of her hair. "Oh. They wanted the floor cleared for the blood drive. Maybe it got tossed into one of those piles over there." She waved her free hand toward the back wall.

"You knew it was mine," Ivy yelled. A few people passing by threw her a look, but she didn't care. "Why didn't you keep it?"

"I'm sorry, Ives, but I've got a little bit more on my mind than your baby pillow."

"It's not a baby pillow."

"I didn't mean it like that, but our entire house is gone." Layla's voice was annoyingly soft. She stood up and took a step closer, like she wanted to comfort Ivy. "We can get you another pillow."

Ivy couldn't listen to her anymore. She definitely couldn't look at her because Ivy was pretty sure she was about to cry. She turned away and headed toward the nearest pile of blankets. They were folded neatly, and she tried to leave them like that, but her hands were shaking, and she couldn't keep herself from tearing through the cotton and wool, praying for a flash of swirly blue.

Her hands scraped at the polished floor, no blue in sight, so she moved on to the next pile. Ivy tried taking some deep yoga breaths in through her nose and letting them out slowly through her mouth, like her mom had started doing when she was pregnant, but Ivy just sounded like a huffing rhino.

Nothing in this pile either. Ivy looked around the room for June, but she was gone and so was her mom. She saw a few other kids from her school, though. Drew Dunaway, one brown arm casted to the elbow, was taking a few sack lunches from a volunteer and slipping them into his backpack. Annie Demetrios, in a pair of bright orange sweatpants, was arguing with a woman Ivy assumed must be her mother because they looked so much alike. Annie looked tired. Everyone looked tired, but everyone was moving, going about their business, and Ivy couldn't get a lock on anyone or anything, no blue pillow in sight. Some people were setting up tables and chairs. Nurses in blue scrubs unpacked a bunch of tiny plastic blood bags.

Ivy's empty stomach lurched at the thought. She saw her dad come into the room carrying some clothes, and he looked so pale that Ivy's stomach jumbled up even more. Dad saw her and waved her over. He didn't smile. No one smiled. There was nothing to smile about.

It's just a pillow, Ivy thought. But it wasn't just a pillow. Her notebook was inside, and those were the only two things she had in the world. Couldn't she just have those two things? Plus, what if someone found her notebook and saw all the things she drew—

Ivy shuddered. She wasn't ready for anyone to see that notebook. She couldn't trust her own sister, much less the rest of the town. She didn't want to think about it. She just had to find her notebook, simple as that.

She kept trying to breathe deeply, but she was doing it too fast and started feeling dizzy. Right when she thought she needed to sit down, Ivy saw a nurse with bright red hair and a stack of pillows in her arms. And in between dingy white and stripes and polka dots, there was a peek of blue.

"Excuse me!" Ivy called, limping toward the nurse.

The woman turned quickly, and the top pillow tumbled to the floor. Ivy picked it up and tried to smile.

"I think you have my pillow," Ivy said.

The woman tilted her head at Ivy. "These were donated by First Baptist."

"No, I know. But that blue one right there"—Ivy tapped the edge of her pillow—"it's mine. My sister accidentally put it in the pile."

"Oh, I'm sorry, hon." She set the stack on the floor and tugged Ivy's pillow out. She handed it over and took the cream one Ivy was holding in exchange. Ivy squeezed her only possession tight and finally breathed a normal breath.

"Thank you," Ivy said.

"No problem. Hang in there." The woman bundled the pile in her arms again and walked off toward the other nurses.

Heading back toward her family, Ivy sneaked her hand into the pillowcase. She just wanted to feel the cool paper of her notebook.

Her fingers reached inside.

And kept reaching.

Her hand found a folded piece of paper, but no

notebook. Suddenly the pillow felt light as air. Too light.

Ivy swallowed a scream and opened the pillowcase wider, nearly sticking her whole head inside. But all she saw was that infuriating drawing of her family she had stuffed into her pillowcase last night before the tornado hit.

Her notebook wasn't there.

"No, no, no." Ivy dipped back into the pillowcase, hoping she'd just missed it somehow, tears gathering like storm clouds in her eyes.

"Hey, you found it," Layla said, suddenly beside her. Ivy didn't even hear her come up. "What's wrong?"

"Nothing," Ivy whispered. She looked around the room, her eyes seeking out every blip of purple and white. It had to be here somewhere. There was no way she could leave this gym without that notebook. Without her hope chest.

"Come on, Ives," Layla said softly. "This is really rough. It's okay if you need to cry."

Ivy wiped her eyes and dragged her teeth over her bottom lip until her eyes were dry and her voice felt steady.

"I'm not crying," Ivy said. "I'm not crying at all."

-⋘◆⋙-

CHAPTER ELEVEN

Displaced

I vy blinked at the hotel room. They were in downtown Helenwood, about a mile from their ruined
house, at the Calliope Inn. The owner, Robin Coyle,
offered a lower price for people displaced by the storm.
That's what Dad called it—*displaced*. Like someone
just needed to come find them and everything would
be okay.

The building was an old Victorian house, and it
was within walking distance of anywhere they might
need to go. Plus, it was more of a bed-and-breakfast, so
they'd be able to use the kitchen and have at least one
meal guaranteed a day.

The room was all dark wood and creaky—creaky
wood floors, two creaky dark wood four-poster beds,

creaky dark wood rocking chair in one corner, a creaky sofa with dark wood armrests in another. Ivy was sure even the TV and minifridge were creaky.

"This is the biggest room we have," Robin said, and she brought in a big plastic box of granola bars, a jar of peanut butter, a loaf of bread, and a bunch of apples and oranges. She set it on the sofa and blew her dark curls out of her face. Her eyes were gentle looking and were the same warm brown as her skin. "I wish there was more I could do. Y'all are going to be pretty cramped in here."

"This is wonderful, Robin, thank you," Mom said, but her voice sounded flat and wispy, as thin as a tissue.

"Let me know if I can help in any way," Robin said and then left.

Ivy's eyes trailed after her. Of course, she'd met Robin once or twice. Helenwood was the size of a thimble, if that, and the Calliope Inn was a historical landmark. The whole town knew Robin Coyle. Her parents had owned the inn before her, and her grandparents before them, and on and on.

Everyone, including Ivy, also knew that Robin only dated other women. Ever since she heard that—Layla had been the one to tell her, in fact, just about a year ago when they ran into Robin at the home improvement store hauling a gallon of paint in each hand—Ivy couldn't help but stare at the woman whenever she saw her around. Ivy's curiosity burned through her like a flame on a match.

"I'm heading back to the house with Jasper," Dad said, his voice jolting Ivy from her thoughts. He handed Evan over to Layla.

Jasper was Dad's best friend from high school and his business partner. They ran a graphic design business in town. "We're meeting the insurance adjuster, and then we're going to see what we can salvage from the house."

"Okay," Mom said. "We need something for the boys to sleep in. These beds are tiny, and you know I'm always nervous I'm going to roll over on them."

Dad nodded and dragged his hand through his hair. Ivy thought everyone looked so weird in their second-hand clothes. Nothing fit right. "I'll come back with something."

"Be careful," Mom said, and then she hugged him. Aaron squawked in her arms, and Dad smoothed his hand over Aaron's head. Dad held on to Mom for a long time, whispering something in her hair. She nodded and when they parted, she wiped her eyes.

Ivy wanted Dad to hug her too, but he just ruffled her hair and told her to be good as he headed for the door.

"Can I come?" Ivy asked.

Dad froze and turned, locking eyes with Mom before looking at Ivy. "Honey—"

"I just want to see it, that's all." Ivy twined her hands together and held her breath. She wanted to go home. She knew it wasn't *home* anymore, but it was all she had. Plus, maybe she could convince her dad to stop by the school again, and she could check if her notebook had shown up in the gym. She felt sick every time she thought about all her stormy pictures lost out there for anyone to find.

"Honey, not today," Dad said. "It doesn't look any different than it did yesterday, and I don't want you to see that any more than you have to, okay?"

Ivy nodded, but it wasn't okay. She kept waiting for all this to just stop, to wake up or for time to reverse or something. Anything so that it wasn't really happening.

Layla came up behind Ivy and ran her hand down Ivy's head, pulling gently on a lock of frizzy hair. Ivy flinched and moved away from her before Layla could even think about braiding it. Ivy knew she was being mean, but she didn't want her sister to comfort her, especially not the way she used to, by playing with Ivy's hair. Because Layla wasn't the sister she used to be, and that's who Ivy wanted. She wanted everything to go back to the way it was. Before the storm, before Layla and Gigi's fight, before the twins. Before, before, before.

Layla didn't say anything, and she and Mom started moving around the room. They had a pile of clothes they got from the elementary school, as well as a bunch of blankets and even some soft toys for the twins. Layla put a few things into drawers while Mom checked the boys' diapers and Ivy just stood there, watching her whole life spill into one creaky little hotel room.

"Ivy, can you change Aaron?" Mom asked. She kissed his head before handing him over.

"Sure," Ivy said.

Ivy found diapers and wipes in the baby bag and got to work. Changing diapers was pretty gross, but Mom didn't usually ask Ivy to do it if it was going to be...well...messy. So most of the time, it wasn't so bad. Ivy just pretended she was changing a doll.

She secured the little Velcro tabs around Aaron's

waist. His skin was soft and smelled like rain and baby powder. He whined a little, and Ivy did her monkey face at him, puffing out her cheeks and pulling on her ears. He immediately stopped and giggled. Ivy tickled his belly before snapping up his onesie. He gave her a gummy grin so cute that she felt guilty for wishing him away a few minutes ago.

"Mom?" Ivy asked.

"Hmm?" She was shaking out the onesies they got from the school and checking their sizes.

"Do you want me to go to the store and get anything for you? Milk and shampoo and stuff like that? Or maybe some art stuff? You know, to use when you start your next Harriet book? It might be a good distraction..."

She trailed off as Layla shot her a weird look. Ivy winced. It wasn't like writing books and drawing were high on Mom's priority list right now. Still, Ivy had to get out of here and look for her notebook. And if Ivy was able to get something her mom needed anyway, then that was just convenience, not selfishness. Her mom *did* need paper and art supplies. It'd been way too long since Mom worked on Harriet. Ivy missed them—Harriet and her mother.

Her mother sighed. "Ivy, Dad and I don't even have our wallets right now. We have no bank cards, no way to get to our money. Until we figure things out with the bank, we're not getting any nonessentials. Dad will get what we need while he's out with Jasper. Other than that, there's too much else to worry about right now, and art isn't one of them."

Ivy nodded, but her stomach sank to her toes. She decided to give honesty a go.

"Well," Ivy said, "do you think I could go back to the—"

"Ivy, I cannot talk about this right now!" Mom snapped. Then she sank onto the bed. She was facing the window, so her back was to Ivy, but Ivy could tell she was crying. The Aberdeen girls were experts at crying silently, but their shaking shoulders gave them away every time.

Ivy's face burned with shame. Layla flicked a burp cloth in the air and folded it into a neat little square, scowling at Ivy. Ivy waited for her mom to get up, but she stayed there, staring out the window.

It was weird. In a house, you could go into your room by yourself when you were mad or needed to cry. This was one single space, no walls or doors between them, unless you counted the bathroom. Ivy didn't really want to go hang out in the bathtub.

Ivy had no clue what to do, so she took Aaron over to Layla and laid him on the bed in front of them. He grabbed his toes and tried to stuff them in his mouth while Ivy helped Layla fold the donated clothes.

"You're doing it wrong," Layla said, snapping a onesie out of her hands.

"I'm trying to help."

"Then help." Layla folded the onesie in half lengthwise and then down. "Like this."

"Does it really matter?" Ivy asked.

"Yes, it makes it smaller in the drawer so there's more room for other stuff."

"What other stuff?"

"Your stuff. My stuff. Mom and Dad's."

"We don't have any stuff!" Ivy's voice cracked on the last few words.

"But we will. Ivy, you can't be selfish right now."

"*I'm* being selfish? What about—"

But Ivy cut herself off as Layla frowned at her. Normally, Layla was a good sister. Normally, she was Ivy's friend. But normally had been sucked away by stormy drawings and tears and tornadoes.

"Why can't you be nice for once?" Layla asked. "Things are really awful, in case you didn't notice. Do you get that we've lost everything? Everything, Ives. Pictures we can't replace. Mom's art. My lacrosse stuff. Dad's computers. All our furniture. The *house*."

"I know, I get it. I'm not stupid!"

"Girls, please!" Mom said from the other bed, but she didn't turn to look at them. She sat there, one hand on Evan's stomach so he didn't fall off the bed.

Layla sighed and rubbed her temples before picking up another shirt. "I don't know what I did to make you act so mean lately," she said quietly, "but get over it, for everyone's sake."

Ivy's eyes widened. Layla didn't even care what she did or why Ivy was mad, only that she *got over it*. Ivy opened her mouth to say something extra mean—what, she hadn't quite figured out—but she never got the chance because there was a knock at the door.

Robin stood in the open doorway—Ivy guessed Dad forgot to close it on his way out—and she was looking between Layla and Ivy in a way that made Ivy wonder how much she'd overheard.

"Hi," she said, smiling. "I have some clothes that might come in handy. Interested?"

"Oh, yes, absolutely," Mom said, standing up and wiping at her eyes. "Layla, could you go and grab those, please?"

Layla nodded and moved toward the door, but Robin nodded at Ivy. "Actually I wanted Ivy here to take a look at them. They're my niece's. She's about Ivy's size and left them here on her last visit. Is that okay?"

"Me?" Ivy asked. That little flicker of curiosity she always felt around Robin flared bright.

Robin smiled. "Yes, you."

"Of course, thank you," Mom said. She waved Ivy off just as Aaron started up his time-for-a-nap cry. Ivy swore her mother looked relieved to get rid of her for a while.

-‹‹‹◆›››-

CHAPTER TWELVE

Robin

If Ivy was going to draw Robin, she'd use a lot of fruit colors. Tangy tangerine and bright cherry red and deep blueberry. Robin was a little younger than Ivy's mom, and she always wore stuff that had fruit patterns on it, but not in a weird way. In a cool, vintagey kind of way. Today she was wearing dark jeans and a light blue top with little green apples all over it.

It made Ivy hungry.

Her stomach rumbled as she limped after Robin down the stairs. They wove through the big entryway and the library packed with all sorts of dark-colored hardback books, then through a room with a lot of fancy chairs and sofas and crystal lamps, and finally into an office next to the kitchen. It was small, with shelves fixed above a dark wood desk and a floral-patterned armchair in one corner. A window took up one whole wall, and the room was bright, the sun streaming through gauzy white curtains.

"Here you go, Ivy," Robin said, motioning toward a laundry basket full of clothes perched on the armchair. "Danielle's style is pretty simple, but it'll do for now, I think. Take what you like."

"Thanks," Ivy mumbled, and walked over to the basket. There were two pairs of decent jeans in her size, as well as a couple of pairs of leggings and a few cute tunics. There was even a forest-green backpack. Everything smelled fresh and clean and cared for. It smelled homey. Ivy's stomach growled again as she ran her hands over the soft cotton and tucked a few shirts under her arm.

"Be right back," Robin said.

Ivy nodded because she didn't trust herself to say anything. She wanted to sit down with her notebook and pens and draw every T-shirt folded in her drawer at home. Every skirt hanging in her closet. One had little red-and-aqua owls all over it. Mom bought it for her birthday last year. It wasn't fruit, but Ivy thought Robin would like it.

"Find something that'll work?" Robin asked from

behind her. Ivy nodded and wiped her eyes before she turned around, just in case. Since the storm, tears liked to leak out of her eyes without her even realizing it. They were sneaky like that.

Robin stood in the doorway, two plates in her hands. "I was hungry. How about you?"

On the plates, Ivy saw slices of ham and melted cheese between slices of thick multi-grain bread, mouth-watering kettle-cooked potato chips on the side. She knew she probably shouldn't eat without her family, but she was powerless in front of a toasted ham and Swiss.

Robin set the plates down on her desk and moved the laundry basket to the floor, freeing up the armchair. Then she plopped into her desk chair with a sigh and offered Ivy a plate.

"Thanks," Ivy said, sitting down with the clothes still in her lap. She popped a sour-cream-and-onion chip into her mouth, and the salty tang went perfectly with the loud crunch. Pure heaven.

"Thank *you*," Robin said. "It's been a while since I've had a friend for lunch."

They both smiled and dived into their sandwiches. It was so good, it almost made Ivy want to cry or laugh or scream. Or draw it. Yes, she would draw an ever-lasting memorial to this sandwich if she had the paper.

"So, Ivy," Robin said as she finished off the last of her chips. She wiped her fingers on a napkin and sighed. Ivy braced herself for the inevitable *Are you okay? How are you holding up? I'm sure everything will work out.* Blah, blah, blah.

"This whole thing really sucks, huh?" Robin said instead. Ivy nearly choked on a chip. Robin not only said the words, she said them with punch. With a *pop* and a *pow.* Ivy had never heard an adult say anything like that before. Adults were supposed to be calm and collected. They were supposed to comfort you. They were supposed to keep you from seeing how much something actually did suck.

But... maybe not. Because as Robin's words settled, Ivy felt more comforted than she had since the storm hit. Maybe even before that.

"Yeah," Ivy said. "Yeah, it really does."

Robin rested her elbows on her knees and looked at Ivy. "I can't imagine, Ivy. I really can't."

Ivy nodded and shrugged all at the same time. "I can't really either."

"That makes sense."

"What does?"

"Just...not being sure how you feel right now. How to process all this."

If Ivy could draw herself right now, she'd be wrapped in clouds and down blankets, pillows and pastel-colored rainbows. Every soft thing. Again, Ivy could only nod, her throat thick and achy. She didn't know how to process anything lately.

"You know," Robin said, "I come from a big family. Four sisters."

"Really? Are you the oldest or youngest?"

Robin smiled. "Neither."

"Me too."

"I know."

And the way Robin said it, it was like she really did know. Ivy wondered again how much Robin had overheard of her and Layla's arguing, how Mom totally tuned them out.

Ivy took a few seconds to look around the office and get her breath back. Robin let her.

The room was painted a soft blue, what Ivy would call arctic blue, and Robin's desk was big and old looking and covered with lots of picture frames. The same lady appeared in a lot of them. She was taller than Robin, with glossy dark brown hair, brown skin, and eyes the color of a shiny penny. She looked sort of familiar. In all the pictures, she and Robin were smiling, their arms around each other. In one, the woman pressed a kiss to Robin's cheek.

Ivy got a stormy feeling in her full stomach.

"Who... who's that?" Ivy asked, motioning toward the kiss picture.

Robin twisted her body to look at the photo behind her. "That's my partner, Jessa Alvarez."

"Partner? Like, with the inn?"

Robin smiled. "No. She's my girlfriend."

"Oh." That's why the woman looked familiar. Ivy had seen her around town before. Ivy thought she remembered seeing Jessa at last year's Pumpkin Festival with Robin.

"She's a photographer and travels all over, but she lives in Philadelphia," Robin said. "Until next year, that is. We're getting married next March, and she's moving here. She's coming to visit in a couple of weeks. You can meet her."

"Oh," Ivy said again. She stared at the kiss photograph. They both looked so happy, huge smiles on their faces, holding hands, some mountain rising up behind them. Of course she was Robin's girlfriend. A real-life girl with a girlfriend. *Partner with the inn?* Ivy felt like an idiot. A blush crept up her neck and into her cheeks. "I should probably go."

She set her empty plate on the little table next to the chair and stood up. The clothes and backpack in her lap tumbled to the ground, and she bent down to pick them up.

"All right," Robin said, standing. Then she started rummaging in a desk drawer. "First, let me give you—"

"No, that's okay. You've done enough. Thanks for lunch." Ivy backed up toward the door, stuffing the clothes into the backpack. She felt as though she were a dark rain cloud about to drench the earth.

"Ivy, wait—"

She was at the door now, but she bumped into the frame instead of going through the actual doorway. Robin frowned at her. Not in a mad way. More like Robin was baffled.

Ivy turned to go, but Robin touched her shoulder, too gently for Ivy to ignore. Ivy forced herself to face her. Robin's eyes were kind, but also a little sad, and Ivy couldn't make sense of them.

Then Ivy looked down and saw what Robin was holding out to her.

A notebook.

And not just any notebook, but a Decomposition notebook. It wasn't like Ivy's. Instead of purple and white, this one was butter yellow with large butterflies on the cover.

"I remember seeing you around before, your head buried in a notebook," Robin said. "Thought you could use a spare. I have a lot of these lying around. I journal a lot, or I used to before I took over the Calliope for my parents."

"You wrote in a journal?"

Robin nodded. "I started when I was about your age too. I grew up in this house, you know. My first entry was a minute-by-minute account of a ghost hunt in the attic with my best friend, Laurel. It was riveting."

Ivy smiled. "Did you draw pictures too?"

Robin laughed. "I wish! I can't even draw stick people. But I would if I could."

Ivy thought about teaching June how to draw a whale last night. Or maybe it was earlier today. The days were all mixed up, but she felt a little calmer than she did a second ago.

"Do you draw?" Robin asked.

Ivy nodded.

"Well, in that case..." Robin turned and rummaged around some more in her desk drawers. Then she held out a pack of brand-new colored pencils. "They're not fancy, but they color. It's a start, at least."

Ivy took the pencils and the notebook. The thick cover was smooth under her fingers. "Thank you. They're perfect."

Ivy made her way back upstairs, hugging the notebook to her chest like it was full of precious jewels.

Pretty soon, it would be.

Ivy jolted awake to a rumbling sound. At first, she thought it was thunder. Quiet and far off, but still real thunder. Her heart jumped into her throat and choked off a whimper.

Then Ivy realized it was her dad, talking really low. She was lying on the floral-printed sofa in the hotel room, where she had all but passed out as soon as she got back from Robin's office, exhausted. Mom had been asleep on one of the beds, the twins tucked in on either side, and Layla had conked out on the other bed, her arms and legs stretched so wide, there was no room for Ivy.

"...don't want to be separated," her dad was saying now. "I think it's important."

Ivy cracked her eyes open just enough to see her parents sitting on the far bed. Mom was nursing Aaron, and Dad was holding Evan over his shoulder, patting his back. The room was early-evening dim, and Layla was still sprawled out on the other bed.

"Normally, I'd agree, of course," Mom whispered back. "But these aren't normal circumstances. On the phone, Paige said they'd be glad to have her for as long as we need."

Ivy's stomach flipped and flopped like a fish on the beach. Paige was Taryn's mom.

"She just seems so unhappy lately," Mom said.

"Of course she's unhappy, Elise. She just survived a tornado and lost the only home she's ever known."

Mom sighed and stroked Aaron's head. "I mean before all this. You know it's true, honey."

Dad scrubbed his face and shook his head.

"Maybe she'd deal with all this better with her friend," Mom added. "For now."

"But for how long?" Dad said. "We can't afford to rent an apartment right now. The rebuild is going to cost a fortune, and insurance only covers so much."

"Exactly, Daniel. Can you imagine the six of us in this hotel room for that long? Layla and Ivy will kill each other."

Dad exhaled loudly and patted Evan's back some more. "I don't know what's with the two of them lately."

"I think Ivy's having a harder time adjusting to the boys than we thought."

"I can't think about this right now. After seeing the house again, salvaging pretty much nothing...We don't even know what we're eating for dinner."

Mom reached out and squeezed his hand as they sat quietly. Eventually, Ivy thought they started talking again, but by then, the air conditioner had clicked on, and Ivy couldn't make out their words. The sound of her heart trying to bust right out of her chest was all she could hear.

-‹‹‹◆›››-

CHAPTER THIRTEEN

Biggest Secrets

The next day, Ivy had never been so happy to go to school. As she stepped inside the two-story brick building, untouched by the storm, it was the most normal thing in the world. Everything was the same. Smelled the same. Sounded the same. All the same people clustering together and talking about the same things. Inside these walls, it was like the storm never happened.

For about five minutes.

"Ivy, wait up!"

Ivy turned to see Drew Dunaway waving his good arm at her. His black curls flopped into his eyes, and his other arm sported a purple cast.

She looked around for Taryn, but so far Ivy didn't see her. Drew was nice, but he hardly ever talked to her without Taryn around.

"Hey," she said when he reached her.

"Hey, what's up?"

She'd never understood this question. Clearly, school was up. Walking in the hallway was up. Same as Drew.

But Ivy simply said, "Nothing."

"Sorry about your house," Drew said as he fell into step next to her.

"Yeah, you too."

"Oh, mine's not as bad as yours. I mean, we can't stay there right now. We're living with my grandma, but we'll be back in a couple weeks. Your house, though. Totally gone. Wow." His eyes widened, and he shook his head.

"Wow," Ivy echoed, but she grimaced. Obviously, she knew that her own house was totally gone.

"Hey, you should draw a picture of it," Drew said.

Ivy stopped walking and blinked at him. "I should what?"

"A picture. Of the tornado or your house or something. You're always drawing stuff in class and at lunch. Remember that Star Wars picture you drew on my lunch bag last month? That BB-8 was perfect!"

"Oh...I..."

"Could I see some stuff?"

"Some stuff?"

"Your drawings. You're really good. If you do a drawing of the tornado, will you show me? I mean, the storm was freaky, but...I don't know. Maybe you could make something cool out of it."

Ivy nodded, ready for him to leave now. She didn't want to make something cool out of her destroyed house. She wanted to make her house whole again, and that was impossible.

"Well, see you in homeroom," Drew said.

"Yeah, sure."

After he loped off down the hall, Ivy scrubbed both hands down her face. She felt like a volcano bubbling and stewing underneath the surface.

Ivy popped open her locker, happy to focus on schoolwork and history lessons and protractors. She was reaching in to grab her math and social studies books when she saw it.

A drawing.

And not just any drawing.

A drawing that made little lightning bolts flash in her belly.

There was a pink-haired girl and a dark-haired girl holding hands, and they were inside a treehouse, this one in the middle of an apple orchard. Except these apples weren't apples, they were glass orbs lit emerald and amethyst and sapphire from the fireflies that lived inside.

Ivy would know.

She drew it.

It had been torn out of her notebook. Her *lost* notebook. Ivy blinked and blinked at the drawing. She pinched her arm, hoping she was dreaming. She pulled the ends of her hair until it hurt.

Wake up, wake up, wake up.

She didn't. The drawing was still there, propped up against her neat stack of books, one corner drooping from the weight of a paper clip. Ivy pushed herself up against the locker so the metal door blocked her from the busy hallway as much as possible. Then she reached in and closed her fingers around the picture. Clipped to the top left corner was another piece of paper with some words in a typed font.

Ivy ~

This is a really great picture of you.

Maybe you should talk to someone about it.

Ivy ran her eyes over the typed page, but there was no name, no signature, no clue to who might have left this for her. They weren't allowed to keep locks on their lockers, so anyone could've placed the drawing inside. Anyone could've taken one look at this picture—at all the pictures in her notebook—and known the pink-haired girl was Ivy.

Anyone.

Ivy's lungs closed up at the thought of someone paging through her whole notebook, drawing after drawing, secret after secret. She had one picture back, a drawing she loved, but this wasn't how she wanted to find it. No way. This was worse than losing the notebook. This was teasing. This was torture.

"You okay?"

Taryn's voice startled Ivy so badly, she knocked her elbow against one side of the locker and yelped, the pain radiating up her arm. Somehow, she managed to hang on to the drawing and keep it in her locker.

"Yeah, fine," Ivy said, stuffing the drawing into her science folder. Her voice sounded clogged and watery. She cleared her throat before coming out from behind her locker door.

"Oh, did your mom talk to you about living with me?" Taryn asked as she rummaged through her own locker.

"Not yet." It wasn't a lie. Not exactly. Ivy's mom hadn't said one word to *her* about going to Taryn's.

Taryn emerged from her locker with a wrinkled red folder clutched in her hand. She stuffed it into her messenger bag. "Well, ask her about it, okay? Wouldn't it be so fun?"

Ivy nodded. It probably would. Taryn's house was big and clean and quiet, and she always had the best snacks. Better yet, Taryn's dad was an amazing cook. After eating nothing but sandwiches and granola bars for two days, Ivy's mouth watered just thinking about Mr. Bishop's spinach-and-cheese omelets and homemade chicken carbonara pasta. But if Ivy went to Taryn's, it would feel like giving up, like admitting that her family didn't need her right now. Maybe even that they didn't want her. That was worse than peanut butter sandwiches for dinner and sharing a bed with her covers-stealing sister.

In homeroom, Ivy's face burned red the second she walked through the door. There were only four seventh-grade homerooms at Helenwood Middle. The person with her notebook was probably in seventh grade, since they knew where her locker was. Which meant the person might be in this room, right this very minute, watching Ivy and waiting. For what, Ivy didn't really know. All she knew was that someone had all her secrets and was hoarding them like diamonds.

She slunk down in her chair as Ms. Lafontaine called roll. All those names, all those faces—it could be anyone. There were a lot of kids at the gym yesterday, some who were displaced by the storm, like Ivy and Drew, and some who were there helping, like June.

Ivy looked at June, who was a few rows up and over. She was hunched over a piece of paper, her head bent low to the desk, pencil moving. Ivy wondered if she was drawing.

"Okay, everyone, a few announcements before we head to first period," Ms. Lafontaine said while she wrote on the Smart Board. Then she tapped the word she'd written with the pen. "*Resilient*. Who can tell me what that means?"

Nobody raised a hand.

"Here's a clue," Ms. Lafontaine said, turning back to the board.

The community was highly
spirited and resilient,
despite the storm damage.

"Any takers now?" Ms. Lafontaine asked.

June's hand shot up.

"Yes, June?"

"I like this word," June said, her hands fluttering around while she talked. "It means able to bounce back."

"Exactly," Ms. Lafontaine said, pointing her pen at June. "*Resilient* means the ability to withstand or recover quickly from difficulties. It doesn't mean things aren't hard. It doesn't mean we aren't hurt. It just means we keep going. We keep living. We keep trying."

June nodded her head like she was at a concert of

her favorite band. Everyone else just kind of sat there, bored, including Ivy. She felt anything but resilient these days.

"Are you talking about the tornado?" Drew asked.

"That's exactly what I'm talking about," Ms. Lafontaine said. "Our school, the elementary school, and the high school are coming together to put on a creative arts show. In one month, on May fifteenth, we're going to display original student art that represents resiliency at the Kellerman Gallery here in town. It can be any kind of art you want, and it doesn't have to be directly related to the storm. You can write, paint, draw, do a collage, submit photographs—as long as we can see it, it's good to go."

The class started murmuring excitedly. June was wiggling so much, Ivy thought she was going to lift right off her chair.

Ms. Lafontaine passed out an information sheet about the art show. Ivy took the green paper, which read, *Resilient Helenwood: Claiming Our Future, Remembering Our Past*, and stuffed it into her hand-me-down backpack. When she glanced up, June was twisted in her seat, eyes fixed on Ivy. She tapped the green sheet and smiled, tossing Ivy a thumbs-up.

Ivy gave June a small smile back, but something nudged at her, like a finger poking her in the shoulder over and over again.

She thought about how much fun she had with June the other night. Actual fun, when fun shouldn't have been possible. Ivy didn't know June very well, but what she did know, she liked. June was funny and kind and, yeah, a bit quirky, a bit weird, but that's what made her interesting.

And June knew what Ivy's drawings looked like. Not the treehouse ones, but other stuff—mermaids and whales and girls' faces. Ivy was sure that June would recognize her art. More important, June was in the gym that morning. She had been stacking pillows and blankets as they cleared the gym floor for the blood drive, right around the time Ivy had been looking for her notebook.

Now Ivy wondered if June was the keeper of her biggest secret.

---◄◄◄◆►►►---

CHAPTER FOURTEEN

Perfect

O n the way home from school, Taryn wouldn't stop talking.

"...soccer game during PE today. That was the toughest goal I think I've ever made. Did you see? It was a thing of beauty. Even Drew looked impressed, and he's the best player I know. Even with a broken arm..."

Ivy uh-huh'd her way through the conversation, but barely heard a word. She was too busy thinking of the note she'd left in her own locker right before she left school:

Talk about what? And please give me back my notebook.

She'd scribbled it on a piece of paper during third period, then threw it away. Then she wrote it down again in fourth period, erased it during fifth, and finally perfected it in sixth. She half hoped it would remain in her locker, unseen, and whoever had her notebook would leave her alone.

But she wanted an answer. And she wanted her notebook back.

"Ivy, did you hear me?"

Ivy blinked Taryn back into focus. "Sorry, what?"

Taryn huffed through her nose, but smiled. "I said, did you notice Drew's cast?"

"As in...he has one?"

"As in, it's purple!"

"Okay."

"Purple is my favorite color, Ivy. Don't you think it's a sign? Maybe I should do a reading for myself."

Normally, Ivy would've smiled and indulged Taryn's gooey crush, but today it felt like sandpaper on a sunburn.

"Purple is also one of our school colors," Ivy said.

"Yeah, but how often does a guy get a purple cast? I think it's pretty cool."

"Yes, it's cool."

Ivy knew her voice sounded uninterested, but she couldn't help it. Her brain felt stuffed with cotton, no room for anything else. And the scene as they walked down Main Street didn't help matters.

Here and there, Ivy saw shingles ripped off roofs and windows busted right through. The curbs were loaded with tree limbs and trash and ruined things that people had swept from the streets. Ivy's favorite pizza place, Vesuvio's, was demolished, only one brick wall still standing at the corner of Second and Main Streets. Ivy's mouth watered for the meatball pizza she'd never eat again. At least not for a long time.

They slowed to a stop at the intersection of Main and Third, where Ivy needed to keep going straight and Taryn needed to turn left.

"Well," Taryn said, "I guess I'll see you later."

"Yeah, all right."

"You okay?" Taryn asked.

Ivy gritted her teeth. She was getting really sick of that question, and she couldn't keep the crackle out of her voice. "I'm *fine.*"

Taryn frowned but nodded as she turned and left. Ivy watched her walk away. She felt a pinch of guilt, but she didn't know what to do about it. All she could think about was her notebook. And when she wasn't thinking about her notebook, all she could think about was her destroyed home. The Calliope Inn that loomed up on her right like a haunted house, all eaves and gables, was very much *not* her home.

Inside the inn, Ivy climbed the creaky steps to her family's room, bracing herself for a flourish of activity and noise. But when she swung the door open, everything was quiet. Her mom sat on the floral sofa reading an old-looking, clothbound book that must have belonged to Robin. Ivy looked around for Layla, but didn't see her. Then she remembered that her sister had lacrosse practice after school. This morning, Mom had insisted that Layla go, claiming it was important to "keep living." Then Mom and Layla had hugged, and Mom had wiped her eyes, all while Ivy watched from the doorway, half a granola bar stuffed in her mouth.

Now Ivy was glad Layla was "living." Ivy couldn't remember the last time she got some alone time with her mother.

"Hey," Ivy said, dropping her backpack and plopping down on the couch next to Mom. "Where's Dad?"

Mom looked up from her book and smiled. Her hair

was in a messy bun, and she was wearing borrowed sweatpants and a T-shirt.

"Hi, sweetie," Mom said. "He's at work with Jasper, and then he has to go by the house later. The farm. The old place."

Mom scrunched up her brows and frowned, clearly clueless over what to call their ruined house.

"Why?" Ivy asked.

Mom waved a hand. "Boring grown-up stuff. Insurance and estimates."

Ivy nodded and looked around their little room. Aaron was in a bouncy seat they got from their church's nursery, batting at the toys hanging from the bar. Evan was lying on a blanket next to his brother, gnawing on a rubber giraffe.

Ivy's head cleared a little. She tucked her legs underneath her and snuggled in next to her mother. She breathed in deep and, despite the unfamiliar clothes, could still smell her mother's scent, shea butter lotion and a hint of pencil lead.

"I lost my notebook at the gym," Ivy said, playing with the hem of her mother's T-shirt. "The purple one I've had for a while."

"You did?" Mom said. "Oh, honey, I'm sorry."

And someone found it. But I don't know who. It was right there, edging toward the tip of Ivy's tongue, but she couldn't get it out. If she said it, she'd have to tell her mother about the note in her locker, and that would lead to all the pictures in her notebook, and that would lead to a lot of stuff Ivy wasn't ready to trust anyone with.

"Can you redraw the pictures you lost?" Mom asked.

"I don't know." Ivy thought of the picture she'd gotten back today, hoping she'd feel something like excitement or relief, but the only thing she felt was a coil of nerves in her belly. Mom kissed the top of Ivy's head and pulled her closer, running her fingers through Ivy's hair. Ivy let herself imagine they were at home, sitting on the worn brown leather couch in their living room, and there was no such thing as tornados and lost notebooks.

Next Ivy knew, she was curled up all by herself on the couch, blinking sleep from her eyes. The hotel room lamps were glowing warmly and the sky outside the window was starting to dim in the evening sun.

"You were tired, sweetie," Mom said from where she was nursing Aaron in the armchair. Evan was now in the bouncy seat, cooing happily.

118

"Yeah," Ivy said, sitting up and rubbing her eyes.

"Hey, I found something that might make you feel better," Mom said. She shifted and Aaron whined, but she managed to dig a folded piece of paper out of her pocket.

"This drawing is yours, right?" she asked, handing Ivy the paper. "It's so beautiful, sweetie. Maybe it'll help you start a new notebook."

Ivy peered at the picture, and her mouth fell open. It was the drawing of her family that she'd ripped out of her notebook the night of the storm—the one that was most definitely missing Ivy.

"How...where did you get this?" Ivy asked.

Mom frowned and patted Aaron's back. "Don't be mad, honey. Robin offered to throw in a load of laundry while you were sleeping, and your pillowcase was filthy. This fell out when I took it off the pillow."

Ivy looked down, her throat too tight to talk. She knew it wasn't a big deal. It was just a drawing, but it wasn't something she was ready to show anyone, especially not her family. For the second time today, her innermost thoughts were exposed.

"Ivy," Mom said. "This is exquisite."

Ivy's chest loosened a little. "It is?"

"Of course it is. I didn't realize how long it's been since I've seen any of your drawings. Honey, you've improved so much! The lines and expressions on our faces. The unique use of color." Mom nodded toward the picture. "That's more than a drawing. That's a story."

Everything in Ivy felt warm. Because yes, it was a story. Because yes, Mom finally saw it, saw Ivy, saw everything she couldn't get out in words since the twins came.

"It's just perfect, Ivy," Mom said.

Everything in Ivy went cold. "It's … it's what?"

"Can I put it up on the wall?" Mom asked, her blue eyes dancing. "Maybe over the sofa or between the beds where everyone can see it? We need a few things to make it feel more homey in here."

Perfect.

It's just perfect.

Ivy looked at the paintings of flowers and mountain scenes already hanging on the walls. She imagined what Layla would say about her drawing. She'd probably love that Ivy colored the grass pink. Maybe Layla would say it was perfect too. What if Dad gushed over it just like Mom was doing?

Ivy quietly folded the drawing.

"Ivy, honey—"

"I don't want it up on the wall."

"Why not? It's lovely."

Ivy stood up. "Can I go to Taryn's? I told her I'd come over and study."

Mom's eyebrows wrinkled together. "Of course, but I'd like to talk about—"

Aaron's cry cut her off. He bucked against Mom's chest, and his face scrunched up like a raisin. Mom stood up and swayed, trying to quiet him.

"Ivy—"

But then, Layla flung the door open so hard that it banged against the wall. She had on navy blue lacrosse shorts, and she was mad, her hair flying behind her. She all but threw her hand-me-down messenger bag toward the desk, its contents spilling everywhere.

"I hate Mackenzie Everett," Layla spat. "I swear, she has it out for me as captain. She tripped me—actually *tripped* me—during warm-ups, trying to make me look bad in front of Coach Vaughn."

Layla barely took a breath before she launched into more reasons why Mackenzie was the "antichrist in eyeliner." Layla wasn't nearly this moody when she was friends with Gigi. Then again, maybe it was this room, their vanished house. Maybe it was a lot of things.

Aaron wailed on, and pretty soon Evan joined him, and the whole room was nothing but noise and complaining, everyone trying to fit somewhere.

No one noticed when Ivy slipped quietly out the door.

-‹‹‹◆›››-

CHAPTER FIFTEEN

Suspect Number One

Ivy didn't go to Taryn's house. Instead, she marched straight down Main Street toward Cherry, where a bunch of old, renovated bungalows stood in a happy little row across from the park. At the corner, she dug the yellow notebook Robin had given her out of her borrowed backpack. She found the nub of a pencil she'd gotten out of her locker and crouched down, balancing the notebook on her knees. On the first page, across the very top, she wrote a name.

June Somerset, Suspect #1

It was more than a name, Ivy thought as she underlined it twice. It was a mission.

Ivy wanted to run down Cherry Street, but her ankle still smarted a little, so she slapped her notebook shut and forced herself to walk. Plus, she had to play it cool. Calm. Casual.

She was halfway down the street when she realized she wasn't sure which house was June's, only that it was somewhere along this road. She slipped her notebook into the backpack and looked around.

It was still light outside and muggy, like she was walking inside a giant's mouth. Still, it was clear, and a white sliver of moon already hung in the sky. Ivy turned this way and that, hoping for some clue to where her suspect lived, but all the houses looked the same with their wide porches and stone steps, large front windows glowing warmly.

Luckily, her suspect found her.

"Ivy, hey!"

A few houses away from where Ivy was standing, a girl ran down the porch steps and waved her hand.

Ivy waved back and headed toward June. She was dressed in black yoga pants and a light pink T-shirt with her hair pulled back on one side, fastened with crisscrossing bobby pins. There was a tiny braid just over her ear. She beamed, and Ivy couldn't help but smile back.

"What's up?" June asked. "Are you running away?"

Ivy's smile dipped. "What? No. Why would you ask me that?"

June pointed to the backpack hanging off Ivy's shoulders.

"Oh," Ivy said, tightening her grip on the straps. "No. I just..." But Ivy wasn't sure how to finish that sentence. She didn't want to tell June that yes, she was sort of running away, if only for an hour or two. And she certainly couldn't tell June her true intentions: investigation.

June tilted her head at Ivy but didn't ask her to explain. "You want to do something?" she asked. "I'm so bored. My mom had to leave to deliver a baby at the hospital, and I'm not allowed to go anywhere, but maybe we can draw some more? I need to draw a person. Can you help me draw a person? Well, a girl, really. A glass girl, to be specific, and I don't think I can—"

"Breathe, June!"

June took a deep breath, her eyes wide. It was actually really cute, and Ivy had to stifle a laugh.

"Sorry," June said.

"It's fine, I just didn't want you to pass out."

June nodded, but looked down at her feet. Her

cheeks darkened a little, and her teeth worried at her lower lip. Ivy used the few seconds to look for some obvious sign of betrayal, like it would show up as a red mark on June's forehead or arm or something. The only really obvious sign was that June wanted to hang out with someone. Ivy could draw it, the loneliness, a wispy cloud the color of a clear sky just after sunset, all deep blues and purples.

"We can do some drawing," Ivy said.

June's head popped up, a grin pushing out the momentary sadness in her eyes. "Great! I've already been trying some things, but I'm *awful*. I'm so glad you showed up. Not that I only like you because you can draw. I like *you*. I really do."

Ivy laughed and, weirdly, felt a warm blush spill into her cheeks. "Good to know."

She followed June to her front porch, where at least two dozen pieces of paper were scattered over the stone floor, along with about thirty different shades of colored pencils. There was a journal too, with one of those fancy ribbons attached to the spine to mark your place. It was open to the middle, and blue-inked handwriting covered the pages.

"So...what are you trying to do?" Ivy asked, sitting

down and pretzeling her legs. "Did you say you needed to draw a glass girl?"

June nodded and sat across from Ivy. "And you're the perfect person to help. You draw girls perfectly. I'm so jealous!"

Ivy narrowed her eyes at June, but June just grinned back. "Um...thanks," Ivy said, but she decided right then to keep her guard up. She was dealing with a suspect, after all, not a friend.

June waved a hand over the drawings on the porch. "They're terrible, right? And I don't know how to make it look like glass. And I want strong glass. Not breakable glass. Or maybe glass that's in the process of breaking, like the girl is getting out of a cage or something. I don't know yet."

Ivy waited for more details, but June just rested her chin in her hands and sighed at her drawings. Ivy picked up a few papers, all of them with round faces and boxy bodies. In the middle of the mess, she saw the drawing of Greenleigh she'd made the other night. June seemed to be using it as an example. Ivy looked around for more of her own drawings, ones that June shouldn't have.

Finding none, she picked up a nearby sketchbook

and laid it in her lap. "Okay, so, I think you should keep your girl simple."

June scooted over all the papers, plowing through them like a boat through ocean waves, until she was right next to Ivy.

"You want to draw the bottom part of the face first and fill in the hair later." Ivy showed June what she meant, and June nodded along. When Ivy was ready to add a body, she paused.

"Sorry, I'm going to need a few more details about this glass girl thing," she said.

"Oh!" June laughed. "Yeah, I guess that does sound kind of weird."

"Just a little."

June grabbed her journal. Ivy heard her take a few deep breaths, her fingers drifting over the written words on the page.

"So...you know that creative arts show Ms. Lafontaine told us about today?" June asked.

"*Resilient Helenwood*?"

June nodded. "Well, I want to do something for it."

Ivy's mouth fell open. "You do?"

"I know I'm not a great artist like you, but it won't only be drawing. It'll be poetry and maybe some photographs too. It'll be a bunch of stuff. I'm not sure yet, but writing is what I like the best, so I want that to be the main part."

"That's great," Ivy said, and she meant it. Still, something that felt a little bit like jealousy pinched at her chest.

"You should do it too, Ivy," June said, as though reading her mind. "I bet you could come up with some amazing drawings."

Ivy smiled and nodded, that pinch twisting harder. Ivy had never put her drawings on display before, especially since all the things she'd wanted to draw for the past year weren't things she could show anyone. They were lock-and-key diary entries. Putting them in a frame and hanging them on a wall felt like that dream where you walk into school without any clothes on.

"Anyway," June said, "I want to draw a glass girl because of this." Then she slid her journal into Ivy's lap and promptly buried her face in her hands. Ivy picked up the journal and read the neat scrawl:

> Glass feet,
> glass hands,
> glass bones under my skin.

Glass heart,

glass eyes,

glass paper and glass pen.

Glass girl in a glass room,

glass wishes on a glass moon.

Glass daughter, flesh and bone.

Glass dreams in a glass tomb.

Ivy read it again. And then again. And after she'd read it a third time, all she could get out was a profound "Wow."

"Is it awful?" June said from behind her hands.

"What?" Ivy shook her head like she was coming out of a trance. "No way, it's amazing. Beautiful. See, you're good at something. Extremely good."

June's brown eye appeared between two of her fingers. "Really?"

"Really. What does it mean?"

June took her journal back, shrugging as she dropped her gaze.

"You don't have to tell me if you don't want to," Ivy said. "I know it can be hard...talking about stuff."

Ivy's mind whirled like a top over hardwood as she thought of the notebook thief's words. She watched

June for signs of smugness or sneakiness or anything other than the doe-eyed look of wonder June wore right now, but she didn't find them.

"You feel like that too?" June asked.

Ivy nodded.

"I've never let anyone read my poems," June said, hugging the journal to her chest. Then she exhaled so loud, Ivy startled. "That was scary. Ugh. But I did it!" June was back to smiling. "And you said it wasn't awful!"

June was so happy that Ivy laughed, her investigation forgotten again. She tapped her pencil against the sketchbook. "It's the opposite of awful. As for drawing a glass girl, I think if we—"

But her voice was cut off when June slipped her hand into Ivy's and squeezed. A fluttery feeling swept over Ivy, the color a soft and whispery pink in her mind. She'd felt it before, after she and June had drawn all night in the school library.

Happiness. She wished her mom could see her right now because *unhappy* was the last word Ivy would use to describe herself.

But as June grinned at Ivy and pressed their palms together, Ivy's stomach fluttered again. And again, pink upon pink, a little *zing* zigzagging up her arm. It felt different from happiness, but Ivy wasn't quite sure why or how. Whatever it was, it didn't stop when June released Ivy's hand and looked down at the sketchbook in Ivy's lap, ready to create her glass girl.

Ivy gulped and then coughed, using the time to get her stomach to behave.

Before they could do or say anything else, June's mom's truck bounced into the narrow driveway. June popped up to her knees and started grabbing at all the papers, collecting them in her arms in a haphazard bundle.

"Help me, will you?" June asked, panic edging her voice.

The whole thing reeked of secrets, a smell Ivy knew very well, so she didn't bother asking why.

"Put them in here," Ivy said, holding open her backpack. Together, they stuffed all of June's papers into the bag, as well as the art supplies and June's journal.

"Thanks," June whispered just as Dr. Somerset, dressed in light blue scrubs, started up the porch steps.

"Hi, girls," she said.

"Hey, Mom," June said. "How's the baby?"

"Healthy and huge. Almost ten pounds." She tilted her head at Ivy. "How's your ankle, Ivy?"

"Better," Ivy said. "Thanks."

Dr. Somerset smiled and then turned her attention to her daughter. "Did you eat the dinner I left for you?"

June nodded.

"And you took your vitamins?"

June huffed. "Yes."

"Just making sure, honey. And I remember asking you to stay inside tonight and work on homework." She looked at her watch. "It's almost seven thirty, which means you should be in your pj's and reading by now."

June didn't respond, but glared at the ground.

"I'm so glad you came by, Ivy," Dr. Somerset said, "but June needs to get some rest."

"Oh. Okay." Ivy looked at June, who had shifted her glare to her mother. "I'll just—"

"No," June snapped. Like a whip.

Dr. Somerset's eyes widened. "Honey—"

"No. It's not even eight o'clock. I'm *twelve*, not two. I want Ivy to come inside, and I want to show her the backyard. I mean, if she wants to stay."

Ivy had no clue what to say. She did want to stay,

but wasn't sure what was going on here. Dr. Somerset looked just as flummoxed. She and June stared each other down.

"All right," Dr. Somerset said calmly. "Ivy can stay if she's able."

June clapped and started jumping up and down.

"Your parents know where you are, Ivy?" Dr. Somerset asked.

Ivy nodded. She didn't like lying, but it wasn't as if her parents would go looking for her anyway. Plus, she'd asked her mom if she could go to Taryn's. This was...close to Taryn's. Sort of.

"You have an hour," Dr. Somerset said.

"Great, thanks, Mom!" June grabbed the backpack and Ivy's hand before pulling her through the front door. Ivy barely caught a glimpse of the house—all hardwood and cozy sofas and a big farmhouse table in the dining room—before June whisked her right out the back door and into the fenced-in backyard.

-‹‹‹◆›››-

Chapter Sixteen

Hideaway

If Taryn were here and she knew about Ivy's stormy pictures, she would definitely call this a *sign* and whip out her tarot cards.

Because there was a treehouse.

In *June's* backyard.

Ivy stared up at the structure, nestled among the gnarly branches of a giant oak near the back fence. A rough wooden ladder led up to a square house. It had a little door and real glassed-in windows on the other three sides.

"Isn't it perfect?" June asked, pulling Ivy closer. The yard was neatly trimmed, but it didn't have any flower beds or a little vegetable garden like Ivy's house had. Well, like her house *used* to have.

"Yeah," Ivy said, but it came out as more of an exhalation. Because it *was* perfect. She could almost see herself inside, safe and happy and not lonely at all because she was with—

A little lighting storm ignited in her belly.

June marched right over to the ladder and planted a foot on the bottom rung. "Now, technically, I'm not allowed up here. My mom thinks it's *unsafe*"—she hooked finger quotes around the word and rolled her eyes—"but she'll never know."

"Wait," Ivy said. "I don't want you to get in trouble."

June went up another step and glanced down at Ivy. "My mom is overreacting, as usual. This treehouse is totally fine. The people who owned this house before us built it, and I heard the real estate agent tell Mom it was barely a year old. Plus, Mom always takes a thirty-minute shower when she gets home, and her room is at the front of the house. We're good to go."

"But—"

"Come on, Ivy, I want to show you the inside."

Ivy's stomach flickered some more, but she ignored it. The treehouse *did* look pretty sturdy. The ladder didn't even creak when she started climbing. By the time Ivy reached the top, June had the door open and

Ivy spilled inside. The floor was smooth, and a sweet, woodsy scent filled the entire space.

But what really grabbed Ivy's attention was all the stuff.

Clearly, this was not June's first trip into the tree-house. There was a camping chair in one corner and a nest of blankets in another, and several books stacked in a neat pile next to an actual lantern. Granola bars and fruit snacks and juice boxes overflowed from a little basket near the door.

"Wow," Ivy said.

June held out her arms. "Behold, my hideaway. Isn't it glorious?"

Ivy had to admit that it was glorious. Through the windows, she could see the first stars just starting to peek into the sky.

"Your mom has no clue you come up here?" Ivy asked.

"Nope. And she never will if I can help it." June flipped a switch on the lantern and a golden glow filled the room. Then she plopped into the camping chair and stretched out her legs, her hands folded behind her head. "She'd probably have the thing torn down."

"But... why?"

June shrugged, but Ivy could tell there was more to Dr. Somerset's rules about the treehouse. Way more.

Ivy sat in the corner with all the books and blankets. It was a perfect reading nook. She tucked her legs under her and tilted her head at June.

"Are you the glass girl from your poem?" Ivy asked.

June shrugged again, but in a way that Ivy knew the answer was yes. "I don't want to be. That's the point."

Night noises closed in all around them, crickets and a gentle breeze, leaves bumping into each other on their branches.

"My parents got divorced last year," June said. "Mom and I left California to come here. Start fresh, she said. She's just really protective."

"Your dad's still there?"

"Yeah. I barely see him. And it costs too much to fly out there very often."

"Do you miss him?"

June nodded. "A lot. I miss my mom too. I mean, yeah, she's *always* there. Major helicopter parent, but it's like I miss the way we used—"

June sucked in a breath and shook her head. "She's just changed a lot."

Ivy didn't know what to say to that, but she knew exactly how to feel. It wasn't a good feeling, but it was bright and familiar, and it flowed down her arms and into her fingers.

"My mom's changed a lot too," she said. "Since she's had the twins. I feel like I barely see her. And now our house is gone, and everything is awful. We haven't worked on a Harriet story in almost a year."

June started to nod, but then she froze, her eyes widening. "What do you mean, a Harriet story?"

"Oh." Ivy laughed. "Um. My mom is Elise Hart."

June sprang forward in her camping chair and grabbed Ivy's hand. "What?"

Ivy laughed again. "It's true."

"That is the coolest thing I've ever heard! How did I not know this? I thought your last name was Aberdeen."

"It is. Hart was her name before she married my dad. That's the name she uses to write."

"I can't believe my mom never told me. She's your mom's doctor! I feel so betrayed!"

This girl was so funny. "Well, they probably weren't talking about Harriet at her pregnancy appointments."

"No, I guess not, but oh my gosh! This is amazing!"

"I guess—"

"Do you get to help her when she writes?"

"Um, sometimes—"

"Oh my gosh, this is you!" She reached over the edge of the chair and pawed at a stack of books, grabbing a thin, tattered paperback. Ivy recognized it immediately. June opened *Harriet Honeywell and the Mermaids of Hurricane Cove* one-handed and pointed to the dedication: *To my brilliant girls, without whom Harriet would never have been born.*

"Um, yeah," Ivy said.

"Do you write too? I know you draw like her! You're so good!"

"Take a breath, June!"

June sucked in some air and let it out really slowly. "Sorry. I've just never met a real author before. I never thought I would."

"It's fine. I get it." But *fine* wasn't really the right word. Ivy would probably be excited if she met Shannon Hale or Jacqueline Woodson or someone like that, but she just felt so weird about Harriet and her mom lately. She fell silent and pulled her eyes away from the Harriet book. It hurt to see it, like looking at a picture of a friend you don't talk to anymore.

June seemed to get that Ivy felt sad about it. She squeezed Ivy's hand, and Ivy squeezed back. Her belly fluttered and flashed. The feeling was wild and sort of unpredictable, just like a good summer storm. She'd never felt this kind of thing with Taryn or any other friend from school. She wasn't sure what made June so different, but at the moment, she didn't care. This was exactly what Ivy had wanted when she drew her first treehouse picture. Someplace that was all her own, where secrets were safe. Of course, this place was all June's own. But Ivy had a feeling that was exactly what the treehouse was for June too, and she was sharing it with Ivy.

Then Ivy remembered that her secrets weren't safe. That was the whole reason Ivy was there. She'd been so distracted by being happy that she'd totally forgotten.

That bright, fluttery feeling went dark and still. She pulled her hand away from June. "We should probably draw your glass girl," she said.

"Right," June said, her back snapping straight.

"Maybe you should check on your mom. Just in case." Ivy's face burned red as an idea came together, but she hoped it was too dark for June to notice.

"Good idea. Knowing my mother, she's probably disinfecting the bottoms of all my shoes right about now." June sighed and stood up, brushing her hands on her pants. At the ladder, she turned and smiled at Ivy. "Hey. Thanks for coming over tonight. I've never shown anyone my treehouse. Or my poems. It...Well, just thanks." Then she was gone in a flash, climbing down the ladder. Ivy peered over the ledge, inhaling the piney scent of the wood, and watched June disappear into her house.

Ivy's fingertips tingled and her breath came fast and hard, but she pushed June's thanks out of her mind and went to work. She kneeled next to the lantern and unzipped her backpack, dumping out all June's stuff. Most of the papers were just drawings, but the journal was what interested Ivy the most.

Ivy started in the back, flipping until she came to the most recent entries. She felt worse and worse with every page turn. She hunted for her name, for any hint that June was the keeper of her secrets, but nothing dated since the storm said anything about Ivy.

It did say a lot about June, though. Ivy's attention snagged on certain words over and over again. Words like *lonely* and *wish* and *want*.

One poem in particular, written before the storm, intrigued Ivy so much that she read it twice.

> They don't know I watch them.
> I am a spy, a lonely girl with a mission,
> trying to see what I missed.
> They laugh and I want to know the joke.
> Their eyes widen and I want to know the gossip.
> But they're too far away, happy without me.
> They see me, but they don't see me,
> and I am no longer a spy.
> I am a girl tucked in bed,
> hidden away in her cage forever.

It was so pretty and sad. It didn't rhyme, but Ivy knew not all poems did. Free verse is what her language arts teacher called it. She remembered that Emily Dickinson's poems hardly ever rhymed. Or made any sense, for that matter. But they made Ivy feel something. And June's poem did the same thing. Maybe that was what poetry was. Feeling.

Ivy scanned the poem again, noticing the date scribbled at the top. It was barely two weeks old. She had so many questions. Who were *they*? Why did June feel like a spy, and why was she tucked in bed when all she wanted was a friend?

She was so busy rereading and wondering, her curiosity speeding up her heart, she didn't hear the soft footfalls climbing the ladder.

"What're you doing?"

Ivy jumped nearly a foot in the air, and June's journal slipped out of her lap. It knocked over the lantern, which spun and spun on its side so that the whole treehouse seemed lit by a disco ball.

"Oh. Um...nothing," Ivy said, scrambling to her feet and righting the lantern. "I was just looking for that glass girl poem."

June frowned and bent down to pick up her journal. It was still open to the poem June never showed Ivy, the poem Ivy never should have read. June's eyes flitted over the words, her frown growing deeper and heavier.

"I'm sorry," Ivy said. "I didn't mean to see it. I just—"

But she couldn't go on because that was a lie too.

June closed the book and hugged it to her chest. Her lower lip trembled, and Ivy didn't know what to do. June's expression was horrible. Not horrible in an ugly way, but horrible in a sad, lonely way. Ivy never wanted to see that expression again. She wanted to make June smile like she had when they'd first drawn whales in the school library. June had been so happy, and it was such a simple thing, those little cartoon whales. At that very moment, Ivy didn't even care about her own notebook or who had it or who didn't.

"I'm really sorry," Ivy said again.

June nodded. "I think I can manage my glass girl on my own now. Thanks."

"June—"

"My mom's almost done with her shower. I better get inside."

June gathered up all her loose papers into a neat little stack and tucked them inside the journal while Ivy watched. She felt helpless, her cheeks hot with shame.

Without another word, June climbed down the ladder, leaving Ivy all alone in the treehouse.

-‹‹‹•›››-

CHAPTER SEVENTEEN

A Real Girl

That night, Ivy couldn't sleep. When she was sure she wouldn't wake anyone up, she slipped out of the bed she shared with Layla and crept into the bathroom. The only decent place she could stretch out comfortably was in the tub, so she climbed in and pulled the curtain closed around her. She balanced the yellow notebook Robin had given her on her lap, pencil poised.

She couldn't stop thinking about June and what happened in the treehouse. She wanted to make it up to June somehow, even though she knew nothing would ever make up for what she did. A lump stuck in Ivy's throat. She thought about her notebook and how awful Ivy felt that it was out there, being looked at and inspected without her permission.

And she had done the exact same thing to June.

One thing she was sure about: June was not the keeper of her biggest secret. She couldn't be. No one who looked as sad and embarrassed as June had could have left that note in Ivy's locker.

But if it wasn't June, then who was it?

Ivy shook off the thought for now, determined to make things right with June. She let her pencil move on its own. She didn't think. She just drew. She didn't want to draw June's glass girl—that was for June to create—but she did want June to see how Ivy saw her.

As a real girl, no glass in sight.

The lines formed, the curves swooped over the paper, eyes and face and mouth and body. Ivy used the pencils she got from Robin to fill in the color. When she was finished, Ivy was out of breath and her stomach was full of lightning bolts again, but she was smiling too.

She sat back, the cold porcelain of the tub seeping through her borrowed T-shirt, and took in her drawing.

A girl, pixie haired and smiling, was floating above the ocean, rays arrowing out from behind her, where a brilliant red-orange sun was rising. The water was a beautiful turquoise, a color it took Ivy at least thirty minutes to get right, mixing the blues and greens until it was perfect. The girl had her arms and fingers spread, like she was about to hug the whole world. Her legs dangled in the air, bare feet relaxed, a simple white dress flowing around her calves. Despite the rising sun, stars sparkled in the sky next to a crescent moon.

It was June's world. And Ivy wanted anything to be possible inside of it...even a girl who flew above a turquoise sea.

The next morning, after she'd choked down yet another granola bar, Ivy left early for school while Mom was busy wiping Aaron's leaky nose. Dad had already left for work, and Layla was grumbling over the chemistry homework she'd left undone.

Ivy stole down the quiet streets, newly washed in the morning sun. It had rained during the night, a gentle and safe sprinkle that Ivy let lull her to sleep after she'd stayed awake for hours drawing, and now the pavement shined like polished silver.

When she reached Cherry Street, she slowed down. This morning, June's house looked a little different. For one thing, it was sage green with a raspberry-red trim. Ivy was so focused on her mission when she got there yesterday, she could've sworn it was a dull beige trimmed with a slightly darker dull beige like all the other houses. But of course June's house would never be beige.

Ivy tiptoed up the front steps. Everything was quiet. It was early enough that June might not even be awake yet, but Ivy certainly didn't want to get caught. Before she could back out, Ivy took the picture she drew last night out of her backpack and slid it through the mail slot in June's front door.

For a split second, she wished she could take it back. Her stomach felt funny again, like it did yesterday in the treehouse before Ivy had gone and ruined everything. What if she'd ruined everything forever and June never talked to her again? What if June hated the picture? Ivy couldn't remember ever wanting someone to love a picture as much as she wanted June to love this one.

What if…what if…what if…

"Breakfast, June!" Dr. Somerset called from somewhere inside. Ivy stumbled backward. Her feet tangled, and she grabbed the arm of a rocking chair so she wouldn't fall down the stairs. When she righted herself, she didn't waste any time turning around and running to school as fast as her still-sore ankle would carry her.

-‹‹‹•›››-

CHAPTER EIGHTEEN

Crush

June ignored Ivy in homeroom. Or maybe she was just so focused on whatever she was drawing that she didn't notice Ivy. Or maybe she despised Ivy now and hated the picture Ivy drew for her, and their friendship was over and done with forever and ever.

When the bell rang, Ivy didn't stick around to see if June might talk to her. Not knowing was better. Not knowing still meant possibility. Ivy didn't think she could handle June walking right past her and not even saying hi. Ivy made a beeline out the door and sat in her first-period class by herself while everyone else chattered in the hallway for five minutes.

By lunchtime, Ivy still hadn't spoken to June, but

there was a note in her locker. As soon as Ivy saw it, her palms started to sweat.

It was another one of her stormy drawings. In this one, she was with a girl who had white-blond hair, inside a treehouse that was made completely of jewels. Rubies, emeralds, diamonds, and sapphires—the scene sparkled around the two girls. Clipped to one corner of the drawing was a small square of paper. Ivy thought about the question she'd left in her locker the day before—*Talk about what?*—and her hands shook as she reached for the answer. She pressed against her locker as much as she could without actually crawling inside and read the message.

You know what.

Here, an arrow angled down toward the two girls. Except instead of a point on the end of the arrow, there was a heart. A *heart*. It was even colored red. Ivy felt sure she was going to throw up right there. She swallowed it down enough to finish reading the message.

You don't have to be embarrassed.
It's okay. You can have your

notebook back when you talk to
someone about it. I think it will
help.

Ivy blinked and read it again. Her drawings didn't
embarrass her; they confused her. They scared her.
Because she never wanted to draw a boy in those treehouses and she didn't really understand why. Because
she *did* want to talk to someone about it—she had
tried, that night when she went to Layla's room with her
stormy drawing and Layla had broken her best friend's
heart because Gigi didn't think about boys either.

She glanced around the hallway, looking for someone who might be watching her read. Drew was across
the hall, but his back was to her, and he was digging
in his locker. Then again, maybe he was just playing it
cool—he was in the gym that day.

*You're really good. If you do a drawing of the tor-
nado, will you show me?*

That's what he'd said to her, barely minutes before
she found the first picture in her locker yesterday. He'd
been so interested in seeing Ivy's drawings. She narrowed her eyes at him, wondering why he would care
so much.

As though he knew she was thinking about him, he turned around and waved at her, smiling. Ivy didn't smile back. In fact, she scowled. Drew's smile dimmed, and he shook his head before walking down the hall with Miles Brecker toward Mr. Santorini's math classroom.

Seething, Ivy put the drawing back in her locker before she ripped out a piece of paper from her science folder. She scribbled a reply.

Help what? I'm fine. Give me my notebook back.

"Hey, did you see Drew today?" Taryn asked from behind Ivy. Ivy startled and dropped her pencil. What's worse, she dropped the note she'd just written, and Taryn stooped to pick it up.

Ivy yanked it out of Taryn's fingers so fast, Taryn gasped.

"Sorry," Ivy said as she placed her note inside the locker and shut the door. "Just trash."

Taryn flicked her eyes to the locker and back to Ivy. "Are you okay?"

Ivy pushed her hair out of her face and smiled. "Yeah. Of course. Just cleaning out some things from my locker. What about Drew? Is he being nosy?"

Taryn made a face. "Nosy? What? No, he's wearing that Star Wars shirt I gave him for his birthday."

"He wears that shirt all the time."

"Yeah, but the roof on his house is pretty much gone, which means that when he went back and got stuff out of his room to have while he stays with his grandma, he got my shirt."

Ivy thought about all her T-shirts buried under a pile of rubble. If she could have just one back, it would be the kelly-green V-neck with *Lonely Hearts Club* written across it in curly script, after an old Beatles song. Layla gave it to Ivy for her tenth birthday and said the color looked good with Ivy's pale red hair.

Ivy swallowed hard. "So now it's the things-Drew-can't-live-without Star Wars T-shirt?"

"Exactly." Taryn beamed.

Ivy cracked open her locker again just enough to grab her math book, then looked around for June. She wanted June to come around the corner and smile and tell Ivy that she got the picture and that she loved it. And she was terrified June would come around the corner and not even look at her or, worse, tell Ivy she hated the picture.

All these thoughts made Ivy's insides go wobbly.

Maybe that was normal. Maybe Ivy felt all wobbly when she and Taryn first became friends, and she just didn't remember. Maybe it was a different kind of wobbly because they were five years old. Maybe Ivy and June's friendship was just a different kind of friendship, stormier and wilder, just like she'd thought last night.

"...just the first shirt he saw, you know?"

Ivy yanked her attention back to Taryn, who apparently had been talking this entire time. "Sorry, what?"

Taryn sighed. "I said, maybe his mom or dad grabbed the shirt. Or maybe it was just the first one he saw. Or maybe he really wanted the one I gave him. What do you think?"

Ivy blinked at Taryn. That was a lot of *maybe*s. And Taryn was pressing her hands to her stomach like it felt all twisty or something. And her eyes were darting around while she bit her bottom lip, like she was hoping for a glimpse of Drew.

Was Ivy biting her bottom lip? She touched her mouth and felt her teeth. Then she took a deep breath because her stomach was definitely twitchy. And she knew her eyes were just darting around, hoping for a glimpse.

Of a girl.

155

June.

A girl. June was a girl. Ivy was a girl. Ivy was biting her lip and her stomach was twisty over a girl. She opened her locker again, but all she saw was that little heart-shaped arrow on her drawing, pointing at the two girls like an accusing finger.

She slammed the locker shut, her belly full of lightning. But not just her belly—her fingertips and toes, eyes and ears—lightning and thunder and bone-soaking rain and darkening clouds.

"Ivy?"

Ivy sucked in a sharp breath. "Hmm?"

Taryn frowned at her. "Are you okay?"

Ivy nodded, but the storm clouds just kept building and building. "Yeah...I'm sure...I'm sure we can figure things out with Drew," she said. "During lunch or something."

"I should ask him to the dance, shouldn't I?" Taryn asked. "It's only two weeks away, and he's so bummed about his arm and his house; maybe it'll cheer him up! Who do you want to ask?"

"What? Me?"

Taryn nodded and nudged her shoulder. "Come on, you have to go with someone."

"I do?"

Ivy had never cared about the Spring Dance before. Their teachers had announced it back in January, and everyone squealed and started whispering, and Ivy had just sat there in homeroom, feeling weird because she had no desire to squeal or whisper.

Taryn opened her mouth to say something else, but Ivy turned away, telling Taryn that she'd see her in science. Ivy walked down the hall as fast as she could without grabbing anyone's attention. Taryn called after her, but she kept going.

Boys ask girls to dances.

Girls ask boys to dances.

Ivy tried to remember a time when that didn't happen at their school—when it was a boy and a boy or a girl and a girl—but she couldn't.

She barely made it to the bathroom before the first tears started leaking out.

CHAPTER NINETEEN

-«‹‹◆››»-

Too Much

Ivy didn't see June for the rest of the day. Part of her was glad. She couldn't stop thinking about that word. It started with a *C* and rhymed with *brush*, and whenever it popped into her head, June's face was right there next to it. This wasn't like her stormy drawings. The girls in those pictures didn't have names. They didn't have journals full of sad poems, and they didn't smile from ear to ear when Ivy taught them how to draw cute animals and glass girls.

The girls in those pictures were just dreams... questions. June was so very real.

When the last bell rang, Ivy hurried down the main hall and out of the school before she could run into

Taryn. She needed to focus on something other than dances and June and words that rhymed with *brush*.

She needed to get her notebook back.

Which is why, when she saw Drew heading down the sidewalk toward downtown, Ivy decided right then and there to follow him.

Once they were clear of the school, she stopped, ducking behind a giant brick mailbox to dig out her yellow notebook and a pencil.

Drew Dunaway, Suspect #2

She tucked everything back into her bag and continued her mission.

Drew walked slowly, his good hand stuffed into his pocket. More than once, Ivy had to come to a full stop to avoid getting too close. She skulked around bushes and hid behind the skinny trunk of a birch tree, which wouldn't have actually disguised anything if Drew happened to turn around as he crossed the street.

She had no clue what she was doing. It wasn't like she could follow Drew into his house or somehow

rummage through his backpack when he wasn't looking. Still, at least this was doing *something*.

In her mind, Ivy ran through a plan that involved
running up to Drew in a panic, saying that she saw a
potentially lethal bee fly into his backpack.

Drew! Aren't you allergic to bees? she would exclaim.

Yes, I am, Ivy! You saved my life! he'd say.

And then he'd fling off his backpack, and she'd
dump it onto the sidewalk, find her drawings, give
Drew a good tongue-lashing, and then never speak to
him again.

She was reveling in the brilliance of this plan when
Drew stopped walking. Ivy stopped too, freezing with
her arms in a funny position like someone had taken
a picture of her running. She braced herself for him to
turn around, to blow her cover, but he just stood with
his back to her, his head tilted like he was listening to
something.

Then Ivy heard a sound coming from a house down
the street. Squinting, she could tell it was Rachel Den-
ning's house—Drew's grandmother. She was famous
for her gardens, flowers spilling over the front and
backyard, more petals than grass.

It took Ivy a few seconds to realize what the sound was—yelling. Two people, maybe more, arguing.

In front of her, Drew shrank. His shoulders curled around his neck. When he finally started walking again, his pace was so slow that Ivy simply stood still and watched him until he disappeared around the corner of the house, bright pink azaleas clouding the porch.

She knew she shouldn't follow him, but she was on a mission, and she had to see it through.

The yelling got louder as Ivy got closer. The house looked peaceful enough, lots of happy pink, the sweet smell of spring in the air. But as Ivy skulked toward the porch, she started to make out words.

"...think this is easy for me?" a woman shouted. The front door was open, so the voices floated out the screen door like water through a sieve. "This is the first day you've taken off work since the storm, and you watched baseball all day. I'm the one dealing with the roofers and insurance. Not to mention you still haven't found an apartment of your own! I have work to do too, you know."

"I know that, Kate," a man's voice boomed back.

"And lower your voice. Drew will be home from school any second!"

The voices became muffled then, but Ivy could still hear tense mumbling. Her stomach pinched as she peered around the side of the house. There, huddled under a window brimming with bright red geraniums, was Drew. He had his knees pulled up to his chest, and he was wiping at his face with his good hand. It took Ivy a few seconds to realize he was crying.

Inside, the yelling crescendoed again. "You really think this is the time to separate?" the man boomed.

Ivy realized the owners of those voices were Drew's parents. Her stomach tightened even more, and she wanted to go over to Drew and see if was okay. Maybe he hadn't been just asking to see her drawings the other day. Maybe he needed someone to talk to, and Ivy knew what it was like to have a tornado mess up her house and even her family. Ivy shook her head, full of too many thoughts and secrets and worries.

She inched forward a bit, still wondering whether or not she should call out to him, when she stepped on a branch. A *crunch* echoed through the momentary quiet, and Drew's red-rimmed eyes met hers. His mouth fell open, and he wiped one last tear away before

162

he scrambled to his feet. Then he grabbed his backpack and ran, disappearing around the back of the house.

Ivy's face burned with shame. She knew she'd just seen something Drew didn't want her to see.

The yelling came to an abrupt stop, and all Ivy wanted was her mother. She wanted her dad too, and maybe even Layla, and she wanted them all piled on her parents' big bed with the TV playing their favorite Pixar movie, a giant bowl of buttered popcorn among them. She didn't want her family to fall apart like Drew's. What if his parents were separating because of the storm? What if the stress was just too much?

Drew's house was eerily silent now.

Ivy turned and ran all the way back to the inn.

Ivy threw open the door to her family's hotel room. For once, she happily anticipated the chaos, the noise, the mess.

But it was silent as a tomb.

The mess was still there—baby toys and clothes, towels, Layla's lacrosse stuff, a bag of bread, and a jar of peanut butter on top of the minifridge—but her family was nowhere in sight.

Ivy checked the bathroom, but it was cluttered yet empty too.

She slumped down on the bed she shared with Layla, crumpling something underneath her. Ivy pulled it out and saw that it was a note with her name on it.

Ivy~

Dad and I had to take care of some things at the house. The boys are with me, and Layla decided to meet us there after school. We'll be home for dinner. Robin said she'd keep an eye out for you.

Love you bunches,

Mom

Ivy balled up the note in her hand. She wanted to see her house. She wanted to go home. She wanted to do whatever her family was doing without her, even if it was just looking at all they had lost. At least they'd be doing it together. Instead, she was stuck in this overstuffed hotel room, alone.

A knock sounded. Ivy glanced up to find she'd forgotten to close the door and Robin was standing there, her hand on the wooden frame.

"Hey there," Robin said.

"Hi," Ivy managed.

"You want to come downstairs for a snack? I've got some lemonade and fresh oatmeal chocolate chip cookies."

Ivy didn't answer right away. She was glad Robin didn't mention the tears or the pathetic sound of Ivy's voice, but she couldn't imagine eating anything right now, even Robin's famous cookies.

Slowly, Ivy slid off the bed. "Thanks, but...I think I'll go to my friend Taryn's house, if that's okay."

She didn't want to stay at the inn, waiting for her family to return, like some forgotten piece of luggage. She wanted something familiar, and Taryn was almost as familiar as her old room. Taryn wanted her more than her family did anyway. She looked around the room, wondering if she should just pack a bag right now, but she couldn't bring herself to do it. If she stayed with Taryn, her family might really be happy. They might be less stressed and more relaxed. And that would be worse than any missing notebook.

Robin's eyes softened. "Of course. I'll let your mom know."

Ivy nodded and met Robin at the door.

"It'll get easier," Robin said, squeezing her arm.

Ivy wiped her face. This was just something adults said to make a kid feel better in the moment. They didn't really mean it. Plus, Robin had never had her house destroyed before. Robin probably didn't even remember what it was like to be twelve.

"How do you know?" Ivy asked.

Robin pursed her lips, as if she was really considering the question. Then she wrapped her arm around Ivy's shoulder and walked with her down the stairs.

"Because you're loved," Robin said.

-‹‹‹◆›››-

CHAPTER TWENTY

Pondering Mysteries

When Ivy got to Taryn's, her best friend squealed and rushed her into the house, which smelled warm and yeasty, like baking bread. Ivy couldn't help but smile, just to be with someone who was excited to see her.

Taryn's mom, Mrs. Bishop, ended up calling Ivy's mom, asking if Ivy could stay the night, and of course Ivy's mom said yes. Then Ivy and Taryn spent the evening eating thick broccoli and cheddar soup out of Mr. Bishop's homemade sourdough bread bowls and trying on dresses for the Spring Dance in Taryn's huge room. Ivy let herself have fun with it, the idea of dressing up for someone she liked. She didn't let her thoughts stray to June. Instead, she pictured some nameless, generic boy with floppy brown hair and a cute smile. The thought never made that pretty ballet-slipper-pink feeling flutter in her stomach, but Ivy still had fun, and all Taryn's dresses were pretty, if a bit small for her.

Taryn talked a blue streak and brought out her tarot deck, as usual. Ivy drew a Two of Cups, and Taryn clapped happily, claiming it meant the beginning of a new relationship. Ivy just shrugged and smiled so she wouldn't blush, but she ended up blushing anyway. If Taryn noticed, she didn't mention it, but Ivy felt just as uncomfortable when Taryn started mooning over Drew. Ivy wanted to ask if Taryn knew about Drew's parents, but Drew had been crying and then he'd run away—Ivy was almost positive he didn't want anyone to know.

Ivy was tired of secrets. More than once, she opened her mouth to tell Taryn about June and how Ivy might, sort of, maybe have a crush on her. But every time she got close, she thought about Layla and Gigi crying in Layla's room and how Gigi left and never came back.

And Ivy didn't want to cry in Taryn's room right now. She didn't want to leave her best friend's house and never come back.

"Ugh, no, boo," Taryn mumbled into her pillow when her alarm clock *cock-a-doodle-doo*'d Friday morning. It crowed like a rooster from across the room and was so annoying that Ivy wanted to smash it against the wall.

"Can't you get a normal alarm clock?" Ivy asked. She threw the covers off and slipped out of bed, stomping over to Taryn's dresser, where the rooster was screeching. "You know, one that just beeps or something?"

"This one makes me get out of bed," Taryn said, her face still pressed to her pillow. "I never hear the other kind, so Mom got me that devil disguised as a clock."

"It's the worst," Ivy mumbled, slapping the OFF button.

She climbed back into the bed and burrowed into the pillow-top mattress. Taryn's breathing grew deep again, and Ivy knew she should wake her up, but her thoughts drifted to June.

Ivy had loved drawing that picture of June and giving it to her. It felt so good to draw exactly what she wanted and actually show someone. But now, a day later, as the morning light streamed through the windows and made everything bright, Ivy worried about how she still hadn't talked to June since that night in the treehouse. What did June see when she looked at the picture, all the lines and colors Ivy meticulously chose? Did June just see a pretty drawing of herself? Or did she see something else—something that started with a *C* and rhymed with *brush*? Is that why June still hadn't talked to her?

Ivy groaned and rolled over, only to find Taryn watching her with a funny expression on her face.

"What?" Ivy asked.

"Pondering mysteries?" Taryn asked.

Ivy let herself smile. A couple of years ago, Taryn started calling those times when they'd be hanging out and then got really quiet "pondering mysteries." It was never an awkward quiet, but the kind that Ivy liked best. Friendly quiet, like the times they would jump on the big trampoline in Taryn's backyard until their sides hurt from laughing, and then they'd collapse onto the stretchy surface and stare up at the trees in silence. They'd ponder mysteries.

"Pondering a lot," Ivy said.

Taryn smiled, and they got quiet and pondered some more.

"Jellyfish," Ivy said after a few minutes. "Jellyfish

are really mysterious to me. The most poisonous one in the world is the size of a gnat or something."

"Black holes," Taryn said.

"How do people get a tiny little ship into an itty bitty bottle?"

"Wind. You can't see it, but you can feel it."

"Tattoos. An ink drawing under your skin. Weird."

"Boys," Taryn said with a sigh, and Ivy sighed too.

Every single time they pondered, Taryn eventually said this. It was as sure as the sun setting in the west. And every single time, it stumped Ivy. She never knew what to say next. She thought she knew what she wanted to say, though.

Girls.

Girls, girls, girls.

Riddle!

Conundrum!

Mystery primo!

But Ivy didn't think it was really girls that were the big puzzle, and when she opened her mouth, something else came out.

"Me."

Taryn propped herself up on her elbows and frowned. "What do you mean, *you*?"

Ivy pushed the covers back and swung her feet to the floor. Her toes sank into Taryn's plush carpet. "Nothing. Just saying stuff. We should get ready for school."

"Yeah, okay, but..." Taryn sat up. Her bangs were a perfect line across her forehead, even after sleeping. "Ivy, what—"

"Can I borrow something to wear?" Ivy asked. She headed over to Taryn's closet, cursing their stupid pondering tradition, cursing that little word that slipped out of her mouth. Because, clearly, Taryn didn't hear "Me" and think, "Oh yeah, me too." Clearly, Ivy was the only one who confused herself.

"Yeah," Taryn said quietly. "Sure."

Ivy flipped through rows and rows of clothes, hunting for something that fit. She found a heather-gray tunic and rubbed the soft cotton between her fingers. Ivy used to have a dress just like this one, except it was a smoky blue color, like a thundercloud about to burst open.

They got dressed in silence, but it wasn't very comfortable. It was the exact opposite of comfortable. Because inside Ivy's head, it was loud, loud, loud. Inside her head, she was trying to say a lot of things to Taryn, things she didn't know how to say with words.

It was like a foreign language in her brain. Ivy-speak. But she wanted to say something. Something true, something *Ivy*.

"I don't want to go to soccer camp with you," Ivy said. Or rather, blurted.

Taryn froze in front of the mirror over her dresser, in the middle of pulling her hair halfway up, an elastic band twisted around her fingers. "What?"

"The soccer camp," Ivy said. "This summer. I don't want to go. I suck at soccer anyway."

Taryn turned around, her hair falling back into her face. "No you don't."

"Well, I still don't want to go."

"Then why'd you say you did?"

"I don't know." Even though Ivy did know. She might not love soccer, but she loved Taryn. She missed Taryn and the friendship they used to have before boys and girls and crushes and baby brothers. Before mean sisters and disappearing families and tornadoes.

Taryn crossed her arms and looked down at her feet. Her toenails were painted electric blue, the tips chipped. Ivy was pretty sure it was the same polish Gigi painted on the last time they all hung out at Ivy's house a few weeks ago.

"Okay," Taryn finally said.

But if it was really okay, Ivy thought she should also feel okay, and she didn't. She felt like a pumpkin whose innards have been scooped out for Halloween.

When they went downstairs for breakfast, Taryn grabbed a Pop-Tart and told Ivy she had to be at school early.

"I promised Ms. Lafontaine I'd help her file graded papers," Taryn said, throwing her backpack over her shoulder. Before Ivy could offer to come along, Taryn was out the door, leaving Ivy alone with Taryn's bewildered parents and the giant pile of eggs and cinnamon raisin toast they had made for both girls.

-◄◄◄◆►►►-

CHAPTER TWENTY-ONE

Blue Whales

When Ivy got to school, June was standing by Ivy's locker. Ivy blinked a few times to make sure she wasn't dreaming, but it really was June, wearing a dark purple sundress and grass-green leggings.

And she was trying to slip a piece of paper through the slats in Ivy's locker.

Ivy froze. Her heart zoomed around her body.

Before she could think of what to do, the paper in June's hand fell to the floor. June scowled and grabbed it, her eyes meeting Ivy's as she stood back up.

"Oh. Hi, Ivy," she said.

"Um. Hi." Ivy forced her feet to move forward. Her

palms were sweating. She wiped them on her jeans and tried to breathe. But it was hard to breathe when June looked so pretty, and Ivy hoped so much that this note meant forgiveness and that June liked the picture Ivy drew. It was even harder to breathe seeing June in front of Ivy's locker with a note in her hand.

"I was just…I was, um, well…" June puffed out her cheeks and held up the piece of paper. "I wanted to give you this."

Ivy took it, and now breathing was nearly impossible.

"Aren't you going to look at it?" June asked.

"Yes," Ivy managed to say. "I'm going to look at it right now. At this thing you gave me, because you gave it to me." She was babbling. She didn't think she'd ever been so nervous in her life.

June cracked a smile, but said nothing.

Ivy unfolded the paper. On it was a drawing of a little whale. A blue whale. June had colored it an azure blue, and there was a red heart in its middle, taking up half of the whale's body. Right below the whale's tail were some words penned in June's neat handwriting.

Love, June

Ivy's heart leaped into her throat. She felt sick and glittery, droopy and elated. She had no clue which emotion to trust.

"I'm sorry," Ivy said. "For the other night. I shouldn't have looked in your journal."

June nodded. "I'm sorry I didn't talk to you sooner. I was—" She bit her lip and looked away from Ivy. "Well, I was mad and really hurt, and I needed to think through it all, but then I realized I missed you and..."

She kept talking, but Ivy's attention snagged around what June had just said—*I missed you*—and wouldn't let go without a fight. Ivy shook her head to clear it and forced herself to focus.

"...maybe you were reading the poem because you liked it," June was saying, "and you were just curious about me, which, I guess, is sort of nice when I think about it like that."

"I did like the poem," Ivy said. "So much. You're really good. But I know I still shouldn't have read it. I should've just asked."

June nodded. "Well. Thanks for the drawing. It was really pretty. Amazing even."

"Yeah? You liked it?"

"Of course! Who wouldn't? It was magical."

Ivy nearly slumped in relief. "Thanks for the whale. It's really cute."

"That thing took me two hours to get right. Can you believe that?"

Ivy laughed. "It'll get easier."

"Most things do," June said.

As they walked toward homeroom together, Ivy couldn't help but hope that June was right.

The rest of the day went by in a haze. Ivy kept taking the little whale drawing out of her folder and staring at it. During math, Mr. Santorini almost caught her while he was passing out graph paper, asking what Ivy could possibly find more intriguing than linear functions, but she slipped the drawing into her desk right before he got to her row. She vowed to be more careful. After all the other drawings that she'd lost, Ivy didn't think she could take losing June's whale too.

Then right after the final bell, Ivy found another note in her locker. Her heart skittered into her throat and stayed there. The morning with Taryn had been so horrible, followed by an almost perfect morning with June; she wasn't sure how much more she could take. She felt too full, like at any moment she'd over-flow and start crying or laughing but wasn't quite sure which one. But when she saw another one of her drawings—this time the treehouse was made out of silvery blue raindrops and the girls were laugh-ing under a glittering umbrella the color of summer grass—she couldn't help but be glad. It was like see-ing an old friend, even if that friend was delivered by an unknown foe.

Ivy reached inside her locker and unclipped the typed note from her drawing.

```
I'm sorry. I only wanted to help.
I know what it's like to have
something you want to tell your
friends but don't think you can.
If it helps, I think your drawings
are the prettiest I've ever seen. I
look at them every day, wondering
about the girls inside. I wish
you'd tell me. They look happy.
```

Ivy stared at the letter for a long time before she realized tears were running down her cheeks. She still didn't have her notebook back, but for some reason, she wasn't even mad. She felt something warm in the center of her chest, like an open meadow in the summer or a crackling fire on a winter afternoon.

She looked back at the girls in her drawing. They *were* happy. She had drawn herself laughing, her mouth wide open, no embarrassment at all. If she tilted it just right, the dark-haired one almost looked like June.

Or maybe Ivy just wanted her to look like June. Her stomach flipped and flopped at the thought. Is this what a crush felt like? A constant stomachache, a bubbly feeling in your fingertips?

Ivy read the note again, wondering what the keeper of her secret wished they could tell their friends. Ivy's mind flashed to June's poem, to the way June had so clearly not wanted Ivy to see it. A fresh wave of guilt washed over her, but then she skimmed the note again. Whoever this person was, they loved her drawings. They weren't judging Ivy. They didn't think Ivy was weird or wrong. They were just...curious.

Ivy couldn't help but wonder if, just maybe, they were simply pondering mysteries too.

She grabbed a pencil from her bag and scribbled a message on a piece of notebook paper.

They're happy because they're together. They're happy because they can be themselves.

Then she placed the note in her locker and snapped the door closed.

-‹‹‹◆›››-

Keeper

The weekend and the next week passed in a blur of fighting Layla for the bed covers, locker notes, and treehouses. Every day at school, Ivy received another one of her drawings and a message from the person who had her notebook, the Keeper of all her secrets. Every day, Ivy wrote Keeper back, and it felt almost like having a pen pal. Ivy had even stopped asking for her notebook. She told herself she just kept forgetting to add the question into her notes, but really, she liked talking to Keeper—so much so that she missed seeing a new note in her locker over the next weekend. In their letters to each other, Ivy was able to say things she'd never said to anyone before.

Ivy told Keeper about her family and what it was like to be stuffed in one hotel room. She told Keeper that sometimes she wished the twins had never been born because she missed her mom. And then she told Keeper how awful she felt that she felt that way. Ivy even told Keeper about Layla and what a two-faced friend and sister she was. Though Ivy didn't tell Keeper why. *Why* still hurt too much. *Why* was still too scary.

The Monday after Ivy had told Keeper that the girls were happy because they could be themselves, Keeper stopped leaving typed notes and switched to a blocky handwriting in all capital letters that Ivy didn't recognize. Still, anyone could make those kind of letters. She spent hours poring over them in her little corner of her family's room, wondering who could've made those pencil strokes. Hoping she knew who did. By now, she was pretty convinced it wasn't Drew. Keeper didn't talk like Drew at all. She couldn't believe he cared about her drawings. He had his own worries. She tried to talk to him once, to see how he was, but ever since the crying incident at his house, he avoided her like she was covered in boils.

Ivy remembered seeing Annie Demetrios in the gym the day she lost her notebook, but Annie was in eighth grade. Their hall was all the way at the other end of the school, and there was no way Annie knew where Ivy's locker was.

Of course, Ivy had considered the possibility that it might be Taryn, but she didn't think Taryn would have been able to wait for Ivy to talk about the drawings. If she was the one who found the notebook, Taryn would've pestered Ivy for every thought in her head that very first day. Plus, Ivy never even saw Taryn in the gym that morning.

That really only left June, which suddenly made perfect sense. Right after June gave her the whale drawing, Ivy and Keeper started writing more and more notes to each other. It was like that little whale had opened up all these things they wanted to say to each other. The thought made Ivy giddy and queasy at the same time, and she wouldn't let herself think on it for too long. Keeper was just Keeper, and now Keeper had even more of her secrets.

I think I might have a crush on someone. But I'm not really sure.

A GIRL?

Yes.

WHO IS IT?

I can't write down her name!

WHAT DO YOU MEAN, YOU'RE NOT SURE?

What if I just really like her as a friend? She's fun and makes me laugh and she's smart. But that doesn't mean I have a crush on her. Or does it?

MAYBE, MAYBE NOT. BUT DO YOU THINK YOU MIGHT HAVE A CRUSH ON ALL YOUR FRIENDS?

I don't think so. I never even thought about it until I started hanging out with her.

WELL, THERE'S YOUR ANSWER. ARE YOU GOING TO TELL HER?

I don't know. Just thinking about it makes me want to throw up.

SOUNDS LIKE A CRUSH TO ME. ☺

Ivy smiled when she read that, but then she felt nauseated. Why didn't she ever think about this stuff with Taryn or any other girl? Taryn was pretty. Taryn was fun and smart.

Why was June different?

June and Ivy had spent almost every afternoon together, and Ivy still didn't know what to do. Dr. Somerset usually worked until dinner, sometimes later, and the two girls would gather up all their art supplies and a few illicit snacks that Ivy sneaked from the inn, and they'd close themselves in June's treehouse.

June was hard at work on her project for the *Resilient Helenwood* art show, her excitement at nearly nuclear levels. If Ivy drew her, June would be covered in neon, the brightest pink and eye-searing yellow. June's latest additions to her project were photographs, something Ivy knew nothing about.

"This is like one of Emily Dickinson's letters to the world," June said the next Sunday afternoon. She brought an ancient Polaroid camera up to her face, snapping a picture of a pair of grubby ice skates that she had found in her attic and that were at least three sizes too small.

"Your letter is that you like ice-skating?" Ivy asked.

She was splayed on her stomach near the lantern, idly sketching her own face into the yellow notebook Robin had given her. Her fingers itched to make it into one of her treehouse pictures, but she knew she wasn't ready to show June one of those.

That is, if June hadn't already seen them.

"No, you goose," June said, gently waving the square photo through the air. "The letter is that I *could* ice-skate." She kicked the skates aside and positioned a soccer ball in their place. "Or play soccer or act in plays or swim in the ocean or do whatever I want."

"You've never done any of those things before?"

June's face fell.

"I mean, I've never acted in a play either," Ivy quickly added. "But..." She trailed off, not quite sure what to say. Clearly, she'd said something wrong and couldn't figure out what.

"It's no big deal," Ivy finally said, quietly. "If you haven't swum in the ocean before. I'm sure you will one day. Or ice-skate. Or whatever you want."

June nodded. "I've seen the ocean. Just not..." She shrugged and rolled the soccer ball a little with her foot.

Ivy wished June would say more but didn't know how to ask her. Secrets were tricky like that. Now, more than ever, Ivy was sure June was keeping one of her own, something that didn't have anything to do with Keeper or Ivy at all.

Keeper *did* say that they knew what it was like to keep things from friends. But maybe they didn't have to keep things from each other. Maybe they didn't have to be Keeper and Ivy. Maybe they could just be June and Ivy.

Ivy smiled at the thought. She'd just started sketching the first line for a treehouse on her paper when June pulled strange objects out of her canvas tote bag for the next photo.

A tube of lipstick.

A necklace with a silver-and-rose-gold heart locket.

A pair of fancy red high-heeled shoes that were clearly too big for her.

"What's all that?" Ivy asked, pushing herself up to her knees.

June's face turned as red as the shoes. She draped the necklace across the wooden floor in between the lipstick and shoes. "Just ... well ... you know, grown-up stuff."

"Grown-up stuff?"

"Yeah, grown-up stuff. You know, things like cool clothes and"—June lowered her voice and looked around like she was about to spill the world's greatest secret—"love."

Ivy swallowed hard, and her heart kicked into high gear. She watched June position everything just so. As June clicked the photo, Ivy couldn't take her eyes off that locket. It reminded her of the heart arrow that Keeper drew, pointing right at one of her stormy tree-house drawings.

"Don't you think about love?" June asked, then she giggled as she laid the photo with the others. "I know Taryn does."

"Um...I...well..." Words that came easily with Keeper tangled in Ivy's throat. June asked it so casually, like she was asking if Ivy preferred dark or milk chocolate, that Ivy couldn't tell if there was anything behind her question.

Ivy wanted June to be Keeper so badly, tears clouded her eyes. She wanted to talk to someone *real* about everything. But every time she pictured it actually happening, she remembered Gigi crying in Layla's room. She remembered how hurt Gigi seemed and how even Gigi was nervous about telling a real person, and she was sixteen! She remembered that Gigi and Layla weren't friends anymore. Even if Keeper *was* June, there was a big difference between writing words on notes in a locker and saying the same words out loud while looking into June's big brown eyes.

Ivy stared down at her half drawing and tried to breathe. She was panicking. Full-on panicking, and all the comfort she felt from her notes with Keeper melted away like a sugar cube in a cup of hot tea. She was about to make up an excuse for why she had to get home, when a voice shattered the silence.

"June Brianna Somerset!"

June's eyes widened, and her hands flew to her mouth. "Mom!"

Feet sounded on the ladder, and June leaped up, grabbing all her stuff and shoving it into a corner.

"No! Mom, please don't come up here!" June's voice sounded funny, like she was trying not to cry. Ivy struggled to her feet and put her notebook and pencils into her bag just as Dr. Somerset appeared in the tree-house doorway.

"What is all this?" she asked, her hands on her

hips. She swept her eyes through all the stuff in the treehouse—the chair, the blankets, the lantern, the books—her mouth hanging wide open. "I said you weren't allowed up here."

"It's fine, Mom!" June said. She was still scrambling to hide everything. "I'm fine!"

"I decide what is fine and what is not fine, young lady," Dr. Somerset said. She looked tired, as usual, clad in a pair of olive-green scrubs.

"If you had your way, nothing would ever be fine," June said. She straightened her back, her hands balled into fists. Mother and daughter stared at each other for so many seconds, Ivy started to squirm.

"Ivy, I think you need to go home," Dr. Somerset finally said, then winced. "I mean...back to the inn."

Ivy nodded, but June grabbed her hand. "She can stay. *Ivy's* fine, isn't she?"

Dr. Somerset threw her hands in the air. "Of course she is. That is not what this is about and you know it. This is about safety, and right now I need to talk to my only daughter alone."

"I'm always alone, Mom!" June said. Or rather, screeched.

Dr. Somerset stepped closer to June and cupped her face in her hands. "Sweetheart" was all she said, but June's hand went slack in Ivy's.

Soon tears ran down June's face and her shoulders shook. Her face was blotchy and her jaw clenched, like she couldn't figure out if she was sad or angry. Ivy wanted to help. She wanted to take June's hand back and hug her. She wanted to draw June a picture of a blue whale with a big red heart in its middle.

"Please," June said, her voice muffled against her mother's chest. "Don't take it all away."

"Ivy, we'll see you later, okay?" Dr. Somerset said softly. She wrapped her arms around June, who was crying so hard that Ivy almost couldn't hear Dr. Somerset, and led her down the ladder.

─❰❰❰◆❱❱❱─

CHAPTER TWENTY-THREE

Reunited

Why had June been so upset when her mom came into the treehouse? Ivy didn't really understand. It was just a treehouse, after all. But then there was that poem she'd looked at without June's permission, and all the photographs June was taking, and her glass girl drawing. June was the loneliest girl Ivy had ever met. Maybe even lonelier than Ivy had ever been. One thing she knew for sure: June needed Ivy just as much as Ivy needed June.

Ivy was lying on her bed at the inn, halfheartedly doing her math homework that was due tomorrow and conspiring how to sneak back to June's, when her dad announced he was taking Mom out to dinner.

"Elise, you need a break," Dad said as he looped an

ocean-blue scarf Mom got from her friend Anna around her neck. "You need to get out of this hotel room, and you need a hot meal. Layla and Ivy are perfectly capable of taking care of the boys."

"I get hot meals every morning," Mom said, yanking at the scarf. She had never left the twins alone with anyone except Dad. "Robin is an excellent cook."

"Okay, fine," Dad said. "You need a hot meal after nine in the morning. And you need to stare wistfully into my eyes and blush when I try to hold your hand."

Mom rolled her eyes while Layla made a gagging sound. Ivy liked it, though. She'd almost forgotten how cute her parents could be. She'd almost forgotten what it was like for her family to joke around.

Dad laughed and ruffled Layla's hair. Then he scooped Ivy from where she was sprawled on the bed and curled her into his arms like he was lifting weights. Ivy squealed, and he blew a raspberry into her hair and laughed.

"Oh, Daniel, really," Mom said. "She's not six anymore."

"What?" Dad asked, pretending to be shocked. "Impossible!" He blew another raspberry and Ivy yelped again, laughing so hard, her stomach hurt. Even though Mom had her arms crossed, she was smiling. It reminded Ivy of *before*. All kinds of befores.

Dad tossed Ivy onto the bed and winked at her before picking up Evan and kissing him on the head. Mom rattled off details to Layla about the twins' bedtime routine and how to warm the bottles in the bottle warmer Dad bought last week.

"And make sure you use the Butt Paste on Evan when you change his diaper," Mom said, and Ivy giggled.

"I know all this, Mom," Layla said, holding Aaron and patting him on the back while he fussed. Ivy took Evan from Dad and made faces at her brother.

"I know you do, sweetie," Mom said, "but two babies are a lot, and Aaron's had a little cold and—"

"Exactly," Dad said, and before Mom could protest anymore, he swept her out of the room. Literally. He swooped her into his arms just like he'd done with Ivy and carried her out the door. She squealed and smacked his back, but she was laughing, which was a pretty nice sound, Ivy had to admit.

"Thank goodness, I thought they'd never leave," Layla said. She walked over to the window and pulled back the lacy curtain. "And . . . we have liftoff."

"They were acting gross," Ivy said, but she and Layla both knew she didn't mean it.

"We're going bananas in this hotel room."

Ivy looked around their tiny home. Not only were the six of them stuffed into one room, but there was all the stuff they'd gotten since the storm. Aaron's and Evan's bassinets, a bouncy seat, secondhand toys, all Layla's lacrosse gear that she'd borrowed from her coach, Dad's work papers he brought home to do here so Mom could get a break sometimes when Layla was at school, Tupperware bins full of diapers and baby wipes and jars of peanut butter and granola bars and canned soup.

Layla checked the time on the phone Dad bought her the other day—Ivy still didn't have one—and then grabbed a tissue to wipe Aaron's runny nose. "It'll be better when we move into that guesthouse."

Ivy stopped making faces at Evan and stared at her sister. "What guesthouse?"

"At Jasper's mom's house? Mom and Dad told us about it a while ago."

"No, they didn't."

"Yes, they did."

"No, they didn't."

Layla made a frustrated sound through her nose and

set Aaron in the bouncy seat. "Yes, they did. It was right after Mom and Dad met with the demolition crew at our house, and they ordered pizza and Mom was worried because Aaron was coughing and—" Layla cut herself off as she pulled the twins' bottles out of the minifridge. "Oh, yeah. That was the night you stayed at Taryn's."

"Yeah, I do remember that." Ivy tried to force a lot of bite into her bark, but really, she felt like her chest was caving in. It wasn't like she was hard to miss in this closet they were living in. Layla didn't even remember she wasn't there?

"Well, anyway." Layla waved a hand, and milk sloshed around in one of the clear bottles. "Jasper's mom lives over on Fifth and has a guesthouse. The dude who rents it right now is moving out next month, and she offered it to us for free. And it has two bedrooms. With actual doors. Amazing, huh?"

"Yeah, amazing," Ivy said, but she was already wondering where she would sleep. Surely, her parents would give Layla a room by herself or Layla would nobly volunteer to share a room with the twins and do the midnight feedings.

Maybe the guesthouse had an attic.

"What's up with you?" Layla asked as she plugged

in the bottle warmer and filled it with a cup of water from the bathroom faucet. "I feel like we haven't talked in forever."

That's because we haven't, Ivy thought.

"Nothing much," she said casually. "Just school and stuff. I'm hanging out with June Somerset a lot lately, so that's cool."

Ivy tried to squash the smile that took over her face, but she couldn't.

"Ah, June," Layla said. She switched bottles and handed the warm one to Ivy. Ivy held Evan like a football and offered him the bottle. He immediately latched on, gulping happily.

"She seems really fun and smart," Layla said.

"She is," Ivy said. Did she say it dreamily? Ivy was almost sure she said it dreamily.

"She's pretty too," Layla went on. "I'd kill for hair like that."

Ivy nodded. She didn't trust her voice not to squeak. June did have pretty hair. It was short, but super shiny, like dark corn silk. She had pretty eyes too. And a pretty smile. And a pretty laugh. And pretty hands. Pretty brain and ideas and heart. Pretty everything.

Ivy tipped the bottle as Evan sucked more milk

down. Her stomach felt fluttery again, thinking about how everything about June was pretty, inside and out. That had to be a sign, right? A sign that she really did have a crush and that June wasn't just some different kind of friend. Ivy's head swam when she tried to figure out the difference.

"Come on, buddy," Layla said as she picked up Aaron and offered him the other bottle. He squawked and squirmed in her arms, moving his head away from her. "You can invite June over if you want," Layla added, totally oblivious to Ivy's roiling thoughts.

"Oh. No...I..." But she couldn't finish because she really wanted June to come over. She thought about what it would be like to sit next to June on the couch and watch a movie on the old TV. She was sure June would like it too, anything to get her out of her own house, which she didn't seem to like very much.

But then, Ivy saw herself reaching out and holding June's hand. And she didn't hold it like she might hold Taryn's or Layla's or even like she'd held June's hand in the past. She tangled her fingers with June's. She ran her thumb over June's knuckle. She sat so close to June that their shoulders pressed together. She—

Ivy forced her brain to stop *thinking*. She felt dizzy

and wanted to cry and laugh at the same time. It was all too much.

"You what?" Layla asked, but before Ivy could think of how to answer, someone knocked on the door.

Layla put Aaron down on a blanket and jogged to the door. Aaron immediately started wailing. Evan was pretty happy, his full tummy poking out like a bullfrog, so Ivy set him in the bouncy seat and scooped up Aaron. He was tense and red-faced, his tiny nose drizzling snot.

Layla flung the door open. Ivy wasn't sure who she expected, but it certainly wasn't Georgia Fitzgerald.

Also known as Gigi.

"Hey, come on in," Layla said, smiling.

Gigi walked into the room, smiling back at Layla. It was a weird kind of smile. A we-haven't-talked-in-forever smile. Gigi was wearing jeans and a flowing tank top, and her hair was plaited into a side braid.

"Hey, Ives!" Gigi said, her eyes lighting up when she saw Ivy. Gigi and Layla were the only two people who called her Ives.

"Hey," Ivy said, but her voice was a whisper. She had no idea what was happening or why Gigi was here right now. She had no idea how she was supposed to feel about it.

Clearly, Gigi had no such doubts. "I've missed you," she said, and immediately pulled Ivy into a hug. Aaron whined between them. Gigi smelled the same, like green tea and flowery shampoo.

"I've missed you too," Ivy said, because it was true. "Where have you been?"

Gigi glanced at Layla, who busied herself folding an already dirty burp cloth. "Just busy. But I'll be around more now, hopefully."

Ivy didn't say anything. Did they make up? Was Layla cool with Gigi being...whatever she was? Was Gigi still with that girl, Bryn? Suddenly, Ivy felt so desperate for answers, she could barely see straight. She wanted to yell and stomp. She wanted to take out all her stormy drawings she'd gotten back from Keeper and line them up for Layla to see. She wanted to show them to Gigi and demand help.

Ivy gulped a few breaths while she tried to get Aaron to take his bottle.

"What's up, little dude?" Gigi squatted down in front of Evan and tickled his feet. Evan giggled. "They've gotten so big."

"Yup, they grow fast," Layla said.

It was all so...normal. Ivy hated it.

Aaron's cry faded to a whimper, and he sucked on his bottle a little. Ivy moved closer to Layla, who was looking at Gigi shake a toy in front of Evan with a little smile on her face.

"Um, Layla, which burp cloth is Aaron's?" Ivy asked loudly, before using her free hand to pull her sister behind a half wall by the beds.

"What's going on?" Ivy whispered.

"What do you mean?" Layla whispered back.

"Why is Gigi here?"

"Why shouldn't she be here? She's my best friend. We're going to hang out."

"I thought you were mad at her." It came out before Ivy could stop it.

Layla's eyes widened. "Why...why did you think that?"

"Because you haven't talked in forever. You haven't mentioned her, and she hasn't come over, and I know that..."

Ivy wanted to say it. She wanted to say it so badly, how she overheard their argument. But the words caught on her tongue like a swear word.

Layla stared at Ivy, her face pale. "Ivy—"

"So what's it like living here?" Gigi asked. Layla

202

shot Ivy one more concerned look before she walked back to the living room area. Ivy followed as Gigi stood up and took a lap around the Aberdeen home.

"Crowded," Layla said. "It's been wild."

Gigi sat on the arm of the sofa in front of Layla. "A tree limb went through our kitchen window during the storm, but that was it. I can't imagine what you're feeling." There was a moment of charged silence, but then Gigi went on. "I'm so glad you called, Lay. How can I help? For real."

Layla exhaled and smiled at Gigi. If Ivy drew her sister right now, she'd use graceful lines and soft pastels, not a hard edge to be found. Layla didn't look at Ivy, even though Gigi just confirmed that they hadn't talked since their argument.

"I'm okay," Layla said quietly.

"How about you, Ives?" Gigi asked.

Ivy opened her mouth to echo Layla, but she couldn't do it. *Okay* was the most useless word on the planet. Instead, Ivy just shrugged. Gigi tilted her head and nodded, like she knew exactly what Ivy meant. She wanted to ask Gigi so many questions. Ivy was full of questions, made of questions.

Gigi came over to Ivy and let Aaron grab her finger while she leaned her head against Ivy's for a second.

Then Gigi pressed a kiss to her temple. It was so gentle, Ivy felt tears sting her eyes.

"Want to watch TV for a while?" Gigi asked Layla, squeezing Ivy's shoulder. "You know, something normal?"

Layla nodded. "Let me just put Evan to sleep."

"Remember when your mom let me put Evan down when he was two months old and I fell asleep while rocking him?" Gigi said.

"You could fall asleep while skydiving."

Gigi laughed. "It's a gift."

Swaying Aaron to keep him calm while he ate, Ivy watched the two best friends. Layla ignored Ivy, but she seemed more relaxed than she had since the storm hit, maybe even before that. For the first time, Ivy noticed how tired her sister looked. She wondered how this whole thing had been for Layla. It'd been hard for all of them, but Ivy never once asked her sister how she was doing.

Layla never asked her either. Not really. It was like they'd forgotten they weren't alone in this. At least, they'd forgotten they weren't supposed to be.

Layla and Gigi whispered to each other while they put Evan to sleep in his bassinet next to Mom and Dad's bed. Ivy struggled to get Aaron to finish even half of his bottle. He fussed and whined, never full-on crying, but never settling down either. Her arms ached from carrying him, and she felt sweaty. His hot little body was like holding a toaster oven. Finally, he dozed off, but every time Ivy tried to put him into his bassinet, he woke up and she had to start all over again. Ivy even tried her monkey face, which got his attention for a whole second before he started crying again. Layla and Gigi settled on the couch and put the TV on a low volume. Ivy thought about asking for help, but she wanted to be able to do this.

Aaron whined louder and Ivy bounced him around the room. Her arm was damp where his little head rested, and even in the dim light, his face looked red. His crying broke into a cough, and Ivy propped him on her shoulder and patted his back. She leaned her head against his and hummed "I See the Moon," a song Mom used to sing to Ivy when she was little.

Ivy pressed her cheek to his, and his skin felt really hot. She shifted him back into the crook of her elbow and felt his head with her hand. He was burning up.

"Layla?" Ivy called, but Layla didn't respond. Ivy walked around their bed and into the living room area. Her sister and Gigi were on the couch, talking. Layla looked up as Ivy got closer and Aaron's cries got louder.

"Will he not go to sleep?" she asked.

"I think he's sick," Ivy said. "He feels really hot. Where's the thermometer?"

Layla's relaxed smile disappeared. She was off the couch in a flash, cupping her whole hand over Aaron's forehead. "He does feel warm. Why didn't you tell me?"

"I *am* telling you."

Layla disappeared into the bathroom and came back with a digital thermometer. "I think Mom put this under his arm yesterday."

Ivy laid Aaron down on the changing pad on top of the dresser and wiggled one of his arms out of his onesie. Layla pressed the tip of the thermometer to his armpit and held his arm down. He screamed even louder, but she kept him there until the thermometer beeped.

The digital display lit up bright red.

"102.9," Layla said. "Oh God, I think that's bad in a baby this young."

"What do we do?" Ivy asked as she fixed Aaron's onesie.

"I'm calling Mom."

Layla took out her phone and tapped the screen, pacing while Gigi looked on, her brows scrunched up in concern. Ivy tried to keep Aaron calm, but he was totally losing it now. She couldn't hear what Layla was saying over the shrieking, but her face looked panicked. She nodded and nodded some more before she finally hung up.

"They're coming, but they want me to take him to urgent care and meet us there."

"How are you going to get there?" Ivy asked. She didn't know where the closest urgent care was, but she was sure it wasn't within walking distance. Especially not with a baby in tow. They had no car. Dad borrowed Jasper's pickup truck to take Mom out.

"I told Mom that Gigi was here and that she could drive me."

"Yeah, of course," Gigi said.

"What about Evan?" Ivy handed Aaron over to Layla and peeked at Evan in his bed. He was totally conked out, oblivious to his twin's woes.

"Mom's calling Robin and asking her to come stay with you," Layla said.

"What? Why? Just let us come with you."

"She's calling Robin," Layla repeated while she grabbed the diaper bag. "Mom doesn't want to have to worry about you and Evan right now, Ivy. Just stay here, okay? And don't wake him up."

And then they left, taking Ivy's screaming baby brother with them.

-‹‹‹•›››-

CHAPTER TWENTY-FOUR

Questions

Ivy curled up on her bed and took out her yellow notebook. She stared at a blank page for a long time. Except for Evan's sleepy baby breaths, the room was silent.

She picked up a pencil and started to draw. She didn't even think. She started making lines, just like her mom taught her.

"When there are too many thoughts swirling around in my head, I let my hand take over," Mom had said a few years ago. "I put a pencil between my fingers, and I let it do the work for me. You'd be surprised what you come up with."

So that's what Ivy did. She couldn't figure out what she wanted to draw, only that she needed to draw to keep back all the thoughts. The quiet made her mind fuzzy with worry, but she kept drawing. Lines, curves, small and large, her hand flew over the page.

Pretty soon, Robin knocked on the door, but Ivy kept drawing. It was like the pencil marks were holding her together.

Ivy heard the door open and the soft pad of feet across the hardwood floor.

"Hi, hon," Robin said.

Finally, Ivy's hand stilled. She looked up at Robin, who was dressed in pajama bottoms covered in pineapples and a plain light gray T-shirt.

"Hi," Ivy said.

"Have your parents called the room?"

Ivy shook her head, her hands limp on her notebook.

"Babies get fevers all the time," Robin said as she walked over and checked on Evan. "I'm sure Aaron's fine."

Ivy nodded and shrugged at the same time.

"Were you drawing? I didn't mean to interrupt," Robin said. She took a step closer to the bed and looked down at the notebook. "That's lovely, Ivy."

Ivy looked at what she was drawing for the first time. It was the profile of a girl's face. Her eyes were staring upward, as though searching for her favorite stars in the sky, and tears were rolling down her cheeks.

Her hair was short and shaded pencil-lead dark, with a single tiny braid curling over her ear.

Robin squeezed Ivy's shoulder and then started digging in her bag, a huge black canvas thing with tiny red strawberries all over it. She pulled out a deck of cards.

"Rummy?" She held up the cards, one eyebrow raised.

"Yeah, okay," Ivy managed to whisper. She closed her notebook, sending June's face into the dark. Layla and Ivy used to play rummy with their grandma before she moved to Florida. Grammy kicked their butts every single time.

Robin handed Ivy the deck, and they settled on the floor in front of the sofa. The cards felt crisp and new and had a bunch of illustrations of lady authors on the back. Ivy spied Emily Dickinson with her hair parted down the middle and pulled into a tight bun.

Ivy dealt them each seven cards, but she couldn't concentrate on the game. She couldn't stop thinking about June, how Ivy just started drawing her face like it was a habit or something. Mom said that sometimes what she drew when she let her hand take over helped her understand herself better. Ivy never understood what her mom was talking about and still didn't. Drawing June like that just made her feel more confused.

Robin flipped cards back and forth in her hand, arranging them just so, and Ivy caught a glimpse of a ring on her finger.

A diamond ring. It was small, but super sparkly; a circle of smaller diamonds surrounded the big one in the middle and trickled down the silver band. It was kind of vintage looking and really pretty. She hadn't noticed it when she was in Robin's office that time.

Robin had more than a crush. She had a whole girlfriend. A fiancée.

"Um, how is...Jessa doing?" Ivy asked, hoping she remembered the name correctly.

Robin flicked her eyes up to Ivy's and smiled. A huge smile that filled her eyes and showed all her teeth. "She's well. Busy, but she'll be here in a couple of weeks."

Ivy laid down three aces, and Robin stuck her tongue out at her.

"Do you miss her when she's not here?" Ivy asked.

Robin nodded. "It's hard, living in two different cities. She travels a lot for work, but I think it'll be easier once she moves here."

"I like your ring."

Robin looked down at her ring and grinned. "Thank you. Jessa actually picked it out herself."

"Did you..." Ivy frowned. How did it work when two girls were getting married? Did both of them get rings? Ivy's head clouded with all the things she didn't know and didn't know how to ask.

"Did I get her an engagement ring?" Robin asked, and Ivy nodded, grateful that Robin seemed to read her mind. "I did," Robin said. "We both wanted one, so we thought, why not?"

"That's nice."

Robin laughed and twisted the ring on her finger. "I think so."

They played a few more rounds, and Ivy ended up winning. While Robin shuffled for a new game, question after question popped into Ivy's mind, stuff she couldn't ask Keeper. How did Robin and Jessa meet? Were their parents fine with everything? Were their friends? Did they ever feel weird holding hands in public? How would the wedding work? Would they both wear white dresses? Would they wear dresses at all?

Robin hummed a little as she dealt the cards. Ivy

picked hers up and tried to focus, but there was one question that kept bubbling up, bigger and bigger, and Ivy couldn't seem to pop it.

"Robin?"

"Hmm?" She laid down a ten, a jack, and a queen of hearts.

"How did you... I mean... you and Jessa... how did you..." Ivy swallowed hard, and her fingers felt sweaty on her cards. When she looked up, Robin was watching her, her hand frozen on the discard pile. Ivy kept waiting for her to fill in the question like most grown-ups seemed to love doing, but Robin just waited.

Ivy sipped at the air, and then she just said it. Well, she whispered it.

"How did you know?"

For what felt like forever, Robin didn't say anything. She didn't even blink, and Ivy felt her face burning. If she drew herself right now, the sketch would be all the reds: dark pinks and mottled crimson.

Then Robin's face changed. It softened, and she sucked in a breath.

"Ah," she said. She picked up a card from the discard pile. "That's a complicated question."

"I'm sorry." Ivy drew a card and discarded another without looking at either one. "You don't have to—"

"No, no. It's fine, Ivy. I don't mind talking about it at all. It's just different for everyone."

Ivy nodded. "What was it like for you?"

Robin folded her cards and set them on the floor. "Well, first of all, there wasn't this one big moment when I *knew*. I was around your age when I really started thinking about it, started realizing that I didn't think about boys like my friends did. I didn't think about them at all except as friends, some of whom smelled bad."

Ivy couldn't help but laugh at that, but it was a jittery laugh. She couldn't tell if she was nervous or excited just to be having this conversation. She wrapped her arms around her legs and pulled her knees to her chest.

"Then, when I was in ninth grade, I met this girl." Robin smiled and shrugged. "And it still took me a while, but around her, I felt...well, I felt awful. Anxious and sick to my stomach. And I stumbled over my words. It was terrible."

Ivy's nerves skipped around her body. "That's how a crush feels, isn't it?"

"Yes, I think it is."

"Did she like you back?"

Robin's smile faded a little. "No. Not as anything other than a friend. But that wasn't her fault, any more than it was my fault that I liked her."

"And after that, you knew?"

"I knew something. What, I'm not really sure. I didn't actually come out until I was a senior in high school."

Come out. Ivy had heard that phrase before, but never really thought about it much until she overheard that conversation between Layla and Gigi. Coming out, the grand revealing where you told your friends and family that you liked girls. Or boys. Or whoever. Where you told them you were different.

"Was it hard?" Ivy asked. "Telling everyone?"

Robin nodded. "Yes. I won't lie to you, it was. I grew up here, and it wasn't easy being a queer girl in a small southern town, much less a black queer girl in the South. It's still hard. I was lucky, though. My parents were and still are very supportive. But I got plenty of heat for it elsewhere. Some people didn't like that I shared a locker room with their daughter or that I still went to church with my parents every Sunday.

Even now, Jessa and I are..." She pressed her mouth flat. "Well, we're just very mindful of where we are and how we act when we're in public. It's not fair, but that's how it is right now. But it's getting better, I hope. We can get married, legally, and that's huge."

Ivy's arms tightened around her legs, and she tried to imagine holding June's hand at school. Like, *holding* holding her hand, their fingers tangled up instead of wrapped around their palms. She tried to imagine telling her parents or Layla. Or Taryn. Or even Robin, right now in this very moment. Anyone with eyes and a mouth and ears, someone more than just blocky words on a page left in her locker. What would they say when she told them?

Suddenly, Ivy was ravenous for more of Robin's story, for anything she could get.

"Did any of your friends freak out?" Ivy asked.

Robin tilted her head at Ivy. "What do you mean?"

"Did any of your friends think it was weird or wrong or something?"

Robin blew out a breath. "Well, I did have a few friends who struggled with it at first. It just surprised them."

Was that what happened with Layla and Gigi? Was

Layla just…working through it all, and now they were back to normal?

"In the end, this was about me, not them," Robin said, tapping her chest. "And the people in my life could either accept that or they could live without me."

Ivy swallowed hard. "Did anyone choose to… well…"

"Live without me?"

Ivy nodded.

Robin smiled sadly. "One friend. And it hurt. It hurt a lot. But if she couldn't love me for me, then I didn't need her in my life. I know that's easier said than done, and it took me a long time to really believe that, but it's the truth."

"What about Jessa?" Ivy asked.

"Well, Jessa's journey is a little different. She didn't come out until she was thirty, just two years ago."

Ivy's eyes widened. "Really?"

Robin nodded. "She's bisexual. Do you know what that means?"

"I think so…that she likes girls and guys?"

"Or anyone," Robin said. "Jessa grew up with a very strict family, so she didn't have as much freedom to question herself or who she might like or might not like."

"Oh."

"You can ask her about it when she visits if you want."

Ivy nodded and chewed on her lip. Her mind was whirling, storming, funneling into a twisting tornado.

"Ivy?"

She lifted her head and met Robin's probing gaze.

"Is there anything particular you'd like to tell me about?"

For a second, Ivy thought she wanted to tell Robin about June and holding hands and Keeper and how she hoped June *was* Keeper and how she was also scared that June was Keeper and how she couldn't figure out what she felt about anything anymore. But she didn't think it was about June. Not really. It was about Ivy herself, and that was the scariest thing of all.

She shook her head and curled into an even tighter ball.

"Okay," Robin said softly. "That's fine. But if you ever do, I'm here."

Ivy nodded, her throat too tight to say anything.

"May I say one thing before I try to redeem myself in the game of rummy?"

"Sure," Ivy whispered.

Robin folded her arms around her legs just like Ivy was doing, like they were two girls sharing secrets at a slumber party. "If a person *was* questioning all this stuff, that person doesn't have to know all the answers. They don't have to be sure about anything. They don't have to label themselves as anything but a human being if they don't want to. Does that make sense?"

"I...I think so."

"That person can just let themselves feel and think about what they need to. It's okay to wonder. To be curious. And it's okay to be sure too. But you—*that person*—don't have to be, all right?"

Something in Ivy's chest loosened. Her arms unclenched from around her legs and fell into her lap. And then that loose thing in her chest made its way up her throat and into her eyes, and suddenly she was crying. Not just crying, but deep, heaving sobs that were almost silent because she couldn't get enough air to make them any louder.

"Oh, honey," Robin said. She scooted closer to Ivy and pulled Ivy into her arms. Ivy went like a boneless fish. Robin smoothed her hand over Ivy's wild hair that her mom hadn't braided in months. Ivy rested her head on Robin's shoulder, hiccuping and not even bothering to wipe her face.

And it felt good.

Ivy was scared and kind of freaking out, but it felt so good just to cry and have a real person hear her.

Then Robin kissed the top of Ivy's head, and Ivy pulled back and wiped her face with her arm, and they went back to playing rummy. Just like that. The world was still here, and Ivy was still here. Robin was still Robin. Ivy's mind was full, and she thought her heart might be trying to beat right out of her chest, but she was still Ivy, questions and wild heart and all.

Ivy glanced at the clock glowing an icy blue on the little table in between the beds. It was barely seven thirty. Layla and Aaron had only been gone for about an hour.

"Robin?" she asked.

"Ivy?" She stacked up the playing cards and slipped them back into the box.

"Do you think I could call a friend to come over for a while?"

Robin smiled. "Absolutely."

CHAPTER TWENTY-FIVE

Sent Away

Robin settled on the sofa with a book, throwing Ivy a wink or a smile every now and then while Ivy and June sat cross-legged on one of the hotel beds. Ivy was certain Robin recognized June from that picture she had drawn earlier, hence all the winking and smiling, but Ivy found she didn't mind.

When Ivy called June earlier, June's voice had sounded small and tired on the phone. But her mom let her walk over to the inn, and she immediately started working on her *Resilient Helenwood* project, pulling papers and colored pencils out of her bag. She didn't seem to want to talk much, but that was fine with Ivy.

She watched June's hand color the little shards of glass she had just drawn an icy blue. The glass girl from her poem wasn't actually made of glass. Underneath all that, she was flesh and bone and smiling and alive. Ivy didn't think she could've drawn the picture better herself. The girl was standing in a large field, bright green grass surrounding her like the ocean, and she had her hands lifted to the sky. Pieces of broken glass were everywhere. In the air and at the girl's fingertips, stuck in her hair and in blades of grass, like she had just broken free.

"This is perfect," Ivy said, swiping her hand over the not-glass girl's face.

June smiled. "It's not as good as your stuff."

"*Good* is subjective. That's what my mom always says, anyway. This is what you meant it to be, isn't it? Which means it's perfect. It's a story."

June stopped coloring and looked up. She stared at Ivy and then back down at her drawing, and then suddenly tears were streaming down her cheeks.

Ivy just sat there, wondering what to do. She shot a glance at Robin, who lifted concerned eyebrows in their direction.

Ivy reached out and took June's hand, palm to palm, no lacing or tangling at all. Just comfort. Just friends.

"I'm sorry," June said, wiping her face with her

free hand. "It's just…this drawing. It *is* perfect, but it's just a drawing, you know? A picture. It's made up. Like you said, a story."

Ivy squeezed June's hand tighter and nodded. No matter how much comfort Ivy got from drawing her treehouse pictures, they were make-believe too.

But maybe they didn't have to be.

"Even made-up stories are about the truth," Ivy said. Her mom had said something like that a long time ago, and Ivy finally knew what she meant. "You could tell your mom. You could tell her how you feel."

"I've tried; she doesn't get it. I'm doing this whole *Resilient Helenwood* thing for her. I just hope she really sees it, you know?"

Ivy nodded again. "June, can I ask…why—"

"Why is my mom such a freak?"

"Um, well, I was going to say why is she so protective?"

June smiled and pulled her hand out of Ivy's. She wiped her eyes with both hands before picking up the blue colored pencil and rolling it between her fingers. It was so quiet, Ivy worried she'd asked the wrong question. Maybe she should mind her own business. Maybe everybody should.

"I was sick," June finally said.

Ivy wasn't sure what she was expecting, but it wasn't that. Surprise mingled with something else, something darker—worry.

"Are you...are you okay?" Ivy asked.

"Yeah, I'm fine now. But my mom worries. A lot. It's like all she does. I think she'd be happy if I never set foot outside ever again. She'd homeschool me if she didn't have to work so much."

June started coloring in a few more glass shards, but then she stopped, staring at the glass girl again. Ivy didn't think June was talking about a cold or strep throat.

"I haven't told anyone this," June said. "I mean, not like I have anyone to tell, really, but I didn't want to be that kid, you know? The cancer kid."

Ivy's stomach sprinted to her feet. "Cancer?"

"I had leukemia. I was diagnosed when I was eight."

"Oh. Oh, wow."

"Yeah. It sucked pretty much all the time for three years. I lost my hair and threw up a lot when I was doing the chemo. I've only been in remission for a year, and my mom is still stressed all the time about it. And she's a doctor, which makes it worse. My body temperature goes up to ninety-nine and she drags me to the hospital."

"Really?"

"And stuffs me with vegetables and organic this and that. I'd kill for a slice of pizza or some chocolate chip cookies. Those granola bars in the treehouse are all I can sneak past her. And now she took all that too."

Well, that explained June's weird lunches.

"I just want to *do* stuff, you know?" June said, her voice small and sad. "That's why I'm going to do the art show. I'm not a great artist, but it's something. I can learn to draw. I can do photography. I can write poems and make a collage. I could've died, but instead I get to have friends and do the things I like."

She waved her hand at Ivy and smiled. Ivy smiled back, but she couldn't get that word—*leukemia*—out of her head. Suddenly, everything about June made sense.

"Is that what that poem was about? The one I read?" Ivy said.

June's face burned bright red and she pressed her hands to her cheeks. "That...that was—"

"You don't have to explain it. Sorry, I shouldn't have even read it."

June nodded. "Thanks. But I want to explain it. That's what friends do, right? They tell each other stuff?"

Ivy's stomach flipped and flopped, a familiar feeling by now, and her mind flashed to her notes with Keeper. "Yeah," she whispered.

"Well, that poem...it was...it was about you and Taryn."

Ivy blinked, trying to remember the exact words of the poem. *They don't know I watch them....They laugh and I want to know the joke....But they're too far away, happy without me.*

"Really?" Ivy asked.

June nodded. "I just...I know I'm a weirdo. I just wanted to know you. You seemed so interesting and fun."

Ivy's heart soared and hurt at the same time. Before she could second-guess it, Ivy threw her arms around June's neck. Right away, June's arms came around Ivy's back, and they sat there together, a little tangle of friendship.

Ivy pulled back first, but kept hold of one of June's hands. "I want to tell you something too." She said it without thinking, not even sure what the *something* was. There were a lot of somethings in Ivy's heart and mind right now, but she wanted June to have something of hers too. Something real, something that wasn't just stuck in a drawing.

"Okay," June said, beaming and clearly relieved. She kept hold of Ivy's hand, and Ivy squeezed so tightly, she worried she might be crushing June's fingers.

But before Ivy could say anything else, a key rattled in the door, and her dad walked in. He looked awful. His hair was a mess, and his eyes were red and droopy looking.

"Dad!" Ivy pulled her hand from June's.

"Hey, sweetie, you okay?"

"Yeah, I'm fine. How's Aaron?"

Dad sighed and dragged his hand through his hair. Robin stood up, and Ivy slid off the bed, June right by her side.

"He's okay for now," Dad said. "He's got an upper respiratory infection, which usually means a bad cold, but the doctor thinks it's bacterial, so Aaron has to go on antibiotics. And because he's so young and they're on the lookout for pneumonia, they're going to keep him in the hospital for now."

"Oh," Ivy whispered. Those words—*bacterial* and

pneumonia—were never good words. Their neighbor, Ms. Clement, had pneumonia once. She was in the hospital for a week. Next to Ivy, June shifted, and Ivy wondered if she was thinking that her mom would probably freak out about the whole bacteria thing.

"But he'll be okay, won't he?" Ivy asked.

"He'll be fine, sweetie," Dad said. "He's in good hands. It'll just take some time." He looked at Robin and smiled wearily. "Thank you so much for staying with Ivy and Evan."

"No trouble at all," Robin said. "I had fun. Ivy's a special girl."

"That she is." Then Dad glanced at June. "Hi, June, how are you?"

"I'm okay, Mr. Aberdeen, thanks."

Dad nodded, but he just kept standing there, running one finger over his eyebrow again and again.

"Well," Robin said, "I'll just go and let you—"

"Actually, Robin," Dad said, "you've done so much already, but I have a favor to ask."

"Of course. Anything I can do to help."

"Thank you. Could you give me one moment with my daughter first?"

"Sure," Robin said. "June, come tell me about yourself, sweetie."

June's eyes met Ivy's, and Ivy swallowed the knot in her throat. All her senses were on alert. June and Robin settled on the sofa as Dad led Ivy over to the beds. He checked on Evan, squeezing Ivy's baby brother's tiny hand, before sitting down on the edge of his bed.

"Honey, I need you to do something for me," he said.

Ivy sank onto the other bed, facing her dad, her heart a bass drum in her chest. "Okay."

Dad looked at his lap and kept touching his eyebrow, a sure sign that he was nervous.

"Dad, you're scaring me."

His head snapped up, and he reached out to take Ivy's hands. "Oh, honey, I'm sorry. It's nothing to be scared of. In fact, you might like it."

"What is it?"

"I know we've been through so much lately. I never expected all this and never, ever wanted you to go through losing your own home. I still haven't really processed it all, and I wanted to keep us together as a family, to figure this out together. But with Aaron being sick and all of us crammed into one room like this...well...your mom and I think it's best if you stay with Taryn for right now."

Ivy slipped her hands out of her father's and balled them in her lap. "Oh."

"Just for a while, honey, until things settle down."

"Are you sending Layla away too?"

"Ivy, we aren't sending you away."

"Is Layla going too?" Ivy's tone sharpened, but if Dad noticed, he didn't say anything about it.

"I have to work, Ivy. We need all the money we can get, and if I don't complete projects, I don't get paid. Layla helps Mom with the boys in the afternoons."

"So, no. You're only sending *me* away. I can help too, you know."

"We're not sending you away," he said again, but quietly. "I need you to be strong, Ivy. This is a hard time for all of us, and we all have to do our part."

And Ivy's part was to get out of the way. To get smaller and smaller. She didn't say any of this, but they both knew it was true. It had been true ever since Mom told them she was pregnant with twins.

At the thought, guilt snapped at Ivy because she really did love Aaron and Evan, but she couldn't help it. She couldn't stop the feeling that she was disappearing from her own family. Mom couldn't even come to tell her good-bye.

"Get some things together to take with you, okay?" Dad said. "I'm going to ask Robin to drive you over to Taryn's. We've already spoken to her mom."

Ivy nodded and got up, drifting through the room to collect her secondhand clothes and her toothbrush. She didn't even have a suitcase to put them in, so she stuffed everything into her backpack. Dad talked with Robin quietly while June hovered nearby, worry all over her face. But Ivy couldn't look at her. Ivy's face flamed up as she finished packing, as June watched her get shipped off.

"Here," June said, handing Ivy the notebook that Ivy had left on the bed. Ivy dropped it into her backpack. Then they just stood there, Ivy staring at the floor. She didn't want June to say anything.

When Dad and Robin finished talking, he pulled Ivy into a hug while Robin and June waited in the hall. He pressed something into Ivy's hand. It was a cell phone.

"I already programmed all our numbers in," he said. "We'll talk every day, okay? And we'll see you before you know it. For your birthday next week, we'll go out to eat anywhere you want, all right?"

Ivy's birthday. With everything going on, she'd barely thought about it, but April 29 was next week.

She'd be thirteen. A teenager. Practically a woman.

"I know it's a special one, and your mom always wanted to do a big party, but..." Dad sighed. "Well, we'll just have to see what we can do. And, hey, you'll already be with your best friend. How cool is that?"

Ivy blinked at him and nodded. Words formed and died on her tongue. Just as well. None of them were very nice.

"We love you so much," Dad said, pulling Ivy into one last hug. "Don't forget that."

Ivy didn't say anything back. Instead, she drifted out the door, barely feeling her feet underneath her.

-‹‹‹◆›››-

CHAPTER TWENTY-SIX

Something Huge

I vy hadn't heard from Keeper in three days. The morning after she was sent to Taryn's, she opened up her locker fully expecting another one of her tree-house pictures and a new note, but there was nothing. She was so mad that she'd slammed her locker door and stomped her way to homeroom without another word to Taryn, who had been chattering away about the Spring Dance coming up that weekend while she rifled through her own locker.

The next day, nothing.

The next, nothing still.

Ivy didn't understand it. She needed to tell Keeper about her family, about being banished, about her talk with Robin, and how with every day that passed Ivy was more and more sure that she liked June. In fact, she was certain. There was too much evidence, too many fluttery feelings and daydreams in math class, and sweaty palms whenever she caught a glimpse of short dark hair in the school hallway.

And she *missed* June. She missed June so much, she felt the ache in her bones. Ivy hadn't seen her outside of school since that night in the hotel room. Apparently, June hadn't actually gotten permission to come over, and now she was grounded for at least a month for sneaking out.

It was awful. It was agony.

And she knew why.

She, Ivy Aberdeen, *liked* June Somerset.

Now she just had to figure out what to do about it, and talking to Keeper was step number one. But as she lay in the middle of the giant trampoline in Taryn's backyard after three days of facing her empty locker, Ivy felt more abandoned than ever.

Everyone was disappearing.

"Okay, are you ready for this?" Taryn said as she started jumping.

"Ready for what?" Ivy asked.

"This!" Taryn jumped harder and higher, somersaulting and flipping, sending Ivy's body bouncing around the trampoline like a rubber ball. Ivy had to stick out her hands to keep from smashing her face into the trampoline. Laughter burst out of Ivy, and Taryn cartwheeled over her, grinning from ear to ear.

Finally, Taryn collapsed at Ivy's side, looping her arm through Ivy's. The movement rolled Ivy into her and their butts collided. They both laughed, but soon they got quiet and stared up at the trees swaying back and forth against the blue sky. Ivy loved laughing, but she loved this too—the easy silence, her best friend so close, she could hear her breathing.

Ivy had been at Taryn's for three days. They'd had fun, watching movies and eating Mr. Bishop's amazing food and doing their homework together. The one thing they didn't do was play soccer in Taryn's backyard like they used to. Ivy kind of wanted to play, but since she told Taryn that she didn't care about the soccer camp, Ivy didn't want to bring it up. Still, being at Taryn's was fine. It was mostly fun. But it wasn't home. Unfortunately, nothing really was.

Aaron came home from the hospital yesterday, but

Ivy's parents didn't say anything about coming home. They sounded stressed every time they talked on the phone, which was every day. She even talked to Layla once, and her sister told her that a guy named Jared had asked her out. Ivy tried to act excited about it, but all she could think about was how easy it was for Layla to tell her that. How easy it was for her to tell Mom and Dad that she had a date or whatever.

Ivy wished her feelings about June were easy.

Mom had been really quiet. She asked Ivy about school and everything, but she always sounded so tired, and one time she had to hand the phone off to Dad because Aaron started crying. Ivy guessed he was still on some medicine and was doing okay, but Dad said Mom was still worried. He didn't really say much about anything else, but he sounded pretty worried too.

Last night, Ivy went downstairs to the Bishops' kitchen for a drink of water and overheard Taryn's parents in the living room talking about the Aberdeens' house.

Or their lack of house.

Ivy didn't get how a lot of the words worked together, things like *insurance claims* and *rebuilding* and *months* and *years*. But one word they kept saying over and over again was crystal clear—*stress*.

Taryn elbowed Ivy. "Pondering mysteries?"

Ivy smiled and nodded, but she didn't continue their game. She didn't know what to say. Her thoughts were nothing but scribble-scrabble on a page and didn't make any sense at all.

Taryn's face fell, and she turned away to gaze back at the clouds. She sighed loudly, and Ivy could tell she'd done something wrong, but she didn't know how to make it better.

"What do you want to do for your birthday on Saturday?" Taryn asked quietly.

"Oh. Um... I don't know."

"My dad will cook you a huge breakfast, obviously," Taryn went on. "You can have your favorite maple-and-brown-sugar pancakes. Then what?"

"I don't know. A movie, maybe?"

"Wrong answer. Nope, try again."

"What's wrong with a movie?"

"You're turning the big one-three! *Teen* is going to be in your age now. It's huge. A movie is one giant yawn."

"Well, maybe I like yawning."

Taryn laughed, and Ivy laughed with her, but she was only half kidding. She was having a hard time getting excited about her birthday.

"The Spring Dance is that night," Taryn said.

Of course it was. "Oh. Well, that's fine. You're going with Drew, aren't you?" Taryn had finally grown tired of waiting around and asked Drew to the dance herself.

"Yeah, but I don't have to go. I can stay with you."

"No way, you've been so excited," Ivy said. "Plus, my parents said they'd take me out to dinner."

Taryn nodded, propping herself up on her elbow. "I wish you'd come to the dance. It'd be more fun with you there."

That made Ivy laugh. "I doubt that."

"Why do you do that?"

"Do what?"

"Like, put yourself down. You're my best friend, you know."

Ivy wrinkled her brows. "I didn't mean to put myself down, I just..." But she didn't know how to finish that sentence. She always felt a little dull next to Taryn, who was all bright colors and bold lines.

"You should come to the dance," Taryn said again. "What if you went with June?"

Ivy snapped her head toward her best friend. "What?"

Taryn cleared her throat. "I mean, it would proba-bly be fun to go with friends, right?"

Ivy stared at Taryn, her thoughts whirling and blinking like fireflies. Because as soon as Taryn said it, Ivy knew exactly what she wanted to do. She was turning thirteen, after all. *Thirteen.* Just the sound of the word in her head made her feel a little more grown up.

A little braver.

A little bolder.

A little more...*Ivy.*

And she might not be with her family right now, but Taryn was right. She needed something huge, something she'd never done before, something wild and scary. Something she wanted.

Ivy knew exactly what to do about her crush on June. She was going to ask June Somerset to the Spring Dance.

By the time Ivy got to June's, she was soaked with sweat. For one, it was unseasonably hot for April, and the afternoon sun blazed over Ivy's back as she jogged down Cherry Street. On the other hand, Ivy was positive she'd be pouring sweat even if it were snowing.

As soon as she decided to ask June to the dance,

Ivy knew she had to do it right away. She tried to act casual as she told Taryn she thought it was a good idea, but inside she was ablaze with nerves. If Ivy thought her stomach was fluttering at the *idea* of crushing on June, that was nothing compared to the reality of actually asking June to a dance. She felt like a whole colony of bats had taken flight in her belly. Thick wings and fuzzy and fanged.

She gulped huge breaths as she rang June's doorbell. She put her hands in her front pockets, then her back pockets. Then she took them out and laced them together in front of her, then behind her. She had just let out a frustrated groan when the door swung open.

"Hi, Ivy," Dr. Somerset said, smiling tightly.

"Hi, Dr. Somerset."

"June can't come out today, but I'll tell her you stopped by."

Ivy gulped again. She knew she should nod and say thanks and go back to Taryn's. After all, Dr. Somerset was a grown-up. But Ivy needed to do this, and she needed to do this now.

"I know she's grounded, Dr. Somerset, but do you think I could talk to her for just a minute? It won't take long, I promise."

Dr. Somerset pressed her mouth flat. "I don't think so, Ivy. I'm not happy with the way my daughter has been behaving lately. Frankly, I'm not sure I want her to see—"

"Mom!"

June appeared behind her mother, and Ivy exhaled.

"June, absolutely not," Dr. Somerset said, turning and pointing to the stairs that led to the house's second floor. "Back to your room."

"Mom, it wasn't Ivy's fault. She didn't know I snuck out."

Dr. Somerset sighed and rubbed her temples.

"Come on," June begged. "She's my friend."

"Fine," Dr. Somerset said, tossing her hands in the air. "Five minutes."

"Thank you, thank you!" June said, and shoved past her mother to get to Ivy on the porch. Before Ivy could offer her thanks too, June slammed the door shut, cutting them off from Dr. Somerset.

"Hey!" June said, launching herself at Ivy, wrapping her in a hug.

"Hey," Ivy said, laughing. She pressed her fingers to June's back, but then made herself pull away. "Listen, I know you have to go, but I wanted to ask you something."

"Okay, shoot." June folded her arms and fixed her attention on Ivy. She was good at that. Whenever Ivy talked, June gave Ivy all her focus. Right now, it was making Ivy sweat even more.

"Well, it's just that…um…" Ivy took a deep breath and made herself look at June, which didn't help the stomach bats. June's short hair was mussed, and her feet were bare. She had on a pair of cutoffs and a periwinkle tank top that made her brown eyes look even darker. She was so pretty. Ivy tried not to think about it too much, but right now, it was all she could see.

"Ivy?"

She blinked and stuffed her hands back in her front pockets. "Sorry. Um. Okay."

June frowned and Ivy knew she was acting weird, so she swallowed a few times and looked down at the stone floor. Maybe if she didn't look at all the pretty, that would help.

"Saturday is my birthday, and I—"

"Oh, it's your birthday!" June said, clapping her hands. "Will you be thirteen?"

Ivy nodded. Swallowed. Breathed.

"I turn thirteen in August, and I'm determined to have a big party," June said. "I don't know if anyone will come, but just having it would be enough, you know?"

"I'd come."

"Of course you would. You're my best friend."

"Really?"

June's smile wavered. "Um...yeah. Is that okay?"

"Yes!" Ivy nearly shouted it, and June startled. "Sorry. I mean, yes. Yes, that's great."

June's smile returned, along with a blush that pinked up her cheeks, and now Ivy was back to thinking about *pretty*.

She shook her head to clear it. "Anyway, Taryn asked what I wanted to do for my birthday, and I thought it might be fun to go to the Spring Dance."

"Oh, yeah! I really wanted to go, but no one asked me, surprise, surprise. Taryn's going with Drew, right?"

"Yeah. So...do you want to go?"

"To the dance?"

Ivy nodded, ready for June to grimace or stammer some excuse. But she didn't do any of those things. Instead, she brightened and bounced on her toes a little.

"Yeah, let's go together," June said. "That'll be even more fun."

It took Ivy several seconds to realize that June had said yes.

"So…yes?" she asked, just to make sure.

"Of course, silly." June laughed, but then grew serious. "That is, if my mom will let me. But even if she doesn't—"

"June, you can't sneak out to go to the dance. I think your mom already hates me."

"No, she doesn't. She's just…she's just being her. But leave it to me." June tapped her chin, her eyes narrowing in mischief. "It's your birthday, and I am not going to let you down."

Ivy grinned and all those bats softened into delicate, beautiful butterflies.

-⫷⫸-

CHAPTER TWENTY-SEVEN

10:33

The day of the dance—the day of Ivy's thirteenth birthday—she woke up with a stomachache, but not a sick stomachache. A nervous, panicky, can't-get-enough-oxygen stomachache.

The past couple of days went by so fast, only two things really stood out. One, she still hadn't heard from Keeper. She had no idea what to think about it all, since June was her only suspect. Her locker was depressingly empty, but the second thing kept her from despairing too much: June's mom had agreed to let her go to the dance. Of course, Dr. Somerset had called the principal and asked if she could chaperone, but still. June would be there.

With Ivy.

At a dance.

With Ivy wearing the most beautiful dress she'd ever seen, thanks to Robin.

Ivy thought about mentioning the dance to Layla when she met her family at a park near the inn Thursday afternoon, mostly because she had absolutely nothing to wear. But what could Layla really do about it? It wasn't like her sister had any dresses to lend her. And since her parents didn't ask her what she wanted for her birthday, Ivy guessed that clothes weren't really in the budget.

Aaron was fussy, so Ivy barely saw her mother for ten minutes. She simply offered Ivy a quick hug and said that she'd see Ivy on Saturday and that she couldn't believe she was about to have "two amazing teenage daughters." Then she went back to the hotel with Aaron, leaving Ivy to eat a picnic dinner with her sister and a sleeping Evan. Dad spent most of the time on the phone with a worried crease between his eyes.

So when Ivy ran into Robin on her way back to Taryn's house, all the details about the dance spilled out. It was like the words were sitting there on Ivy's tongue, waiting for someone to listen.

"That's so exciting, Ivy," Robin had said. "And you're going with...June?"

Ivy nodded, a blush rushing into her cheeks. "I don't have anything to wear, though. I can probably find something at Taryn's, even though her stuff is a little small for me. It'll be fine."

Robin tilted her head at Ivy, her eyes thoughtful. Before Ivy knew it, Robin pulled her into Lacey's, a little boutique kid's clothing shop right off Main Street. Ivy tried on dozens of dresses, none of them feeling quite right.

Until.

Robin found a green dress on the sale rack. But it wasn't just green. It was all the greens. Forest and pine and kelly and grass, all flowing together like a green ocean. The dress was sleeveless and fitted at the waist, but the skirt flared out with a layer of chiffon over satin. A-line, Robin had called it.

Ivy loved it.

"That's the one," Robin said, grinning. "Absolutely perfect with your hair." She asked Ivy to twirl, and they both laughed as the dress flowed around Ivy perfectly.

After Ivy changed, Robin took the dress to the register and paid for it before Ivy could even blink.

"You don't...I don't know when I can pay you back," Ivy said when Robin handed her the bag.

"I don't want you to. I don't want you to worry about it at all. I just want you to go to that dance, be yourself, and tell me all about it when it's over. Okay?"

Ivy swallowed around the balloon in her throat and nodded. Then she hugged Robin, and Robin hugged her back, running her hand over Ivy's hair just like Mom used to. It was so nice to be hugged by a grown-up, by someone Ivy liked and trusted. It was nice to feel taken care of.

Now, the morning of her birthday, Ivy stuffed herself with Mr. Bishop's famous maple-and-brown-sugar pancakes, bacon, and orange juice, daydreaming about her dress. And this felt nice too. Taryn's mom stuck a few candles into Ivy's giant stack of pancakes, and they all sang "Happy Birthday." Ivy cracked up because Taryn was completely off-key, but she didn't really care. She sang loud and proud, and Ivy loved that about her.

Ivy kept watching the clock while she ate, the hands moving closer and closer to 10:33, which was when she was born. At that exact moment, 10:33 in the morning, Ivy's mom always told her happy birthday. If her birthday fell on a school day, Mom arranged for whatever teacher Ivy was with at that time to slip her a note and a little piece of chocolate at exactly 10:33. It was a thing her mom did that she never heard of any other moms doing, and Ivy loved it. Mom did it with Layla too, even though Layla was born at 4:15 AM in October. Every year, Mom set an alarm for herself and went into Layla's room, snuggling with Ivy's groggy and usually cranky sister, and sang "Happy Birthday" like a lullaby.

Ivy was sure Mom would do it with the twins too, every January 16 at 1:46 in the afternoon for Aaron, and then again at 1:53 for Evan. She would have to sneak them notes in school too.

After Ivy unwrapped Taryn's present—a new turquoise messenger bag that Ivy loved, with a nice wide strap and magnetic closures—they settled in front of the TV to watch a movie. They brought a bowl of buttery popcorn with them, even though Ivy was so full, she could barely get a breath.

Ivy clung to her cell phone as the time moved closer and closer to 10:33.

10:14.

10:27.

Then it hit 10:33.

Then it passed.

10:41.

11:03.

And Ivy's phone didn't ring.

Now the clock read 11:33. The movie kept playing, and through the window, Ivy saw Mr. Bishop pushing the lawn mower up and down the front yard. But Ivy couldn't hear anything over the sound of her lungs trying to get enough air while she turned off her phone.

CHAPTER TWENTY-EIGHT

Dance

The school's gymnasium was unrecognizable. Usually, it reeked of sweat and rubber with a hint of cheap fruity body spray. Tonight, it smelled of sparkly red punch and older brothers' cologne and flowers from corsages and whatever those things are called that girls pin onto a guy's jacket. And, yes, there was still a trace of the sweat and rubber, but overall, the place looked magical. White lights twinkled everywhere. They wound around the fake plants set up in the room, draped over the wall clocks and basketball goals, snaked through the bowls of chips and cookies on the snack table. The DJ played a happy song, and kids were already dancing in the center of the room. Everything was soft and pretty.

Including June.

Ivy walked in with Taryn and found June standing by the snack table. Her mom was here somewhere too, but at the moment, that didn't matter. June was wearing a flowing, lacy dress the color of winter sunshine. Her dark hair and eyes looked even darker against the pale yellow. Ivy's stomach did its normal thing, which is to say it thundered and flashed like a wild storm, but for once Ivy didn't mind. She just let it be what it was. Because June was right—some storms could be *awesome*.

Earlier, when Mr. Bishop called up to Taryn's room at 5:51 to tell the girls that it was time to leave for the dance, Ivy still hadn't turned on her phone to see if her parents had called. At lunch when Mrs. Bishop asked if Ivy had talked to them, she had mumbled a yes, embarrassed that her family had forgotten her on the most important birthday she'd ever had.

Ivy had spent the rest of the afternoon doing the only thing that made her feel better: drawing. While Taryn and Mrs. Bishop ran a few errands, Ivy holed up in Taryn's room and drew her first complete treehouse picture since the tornado. Except this time, it wasn't some nameless girl inside the treehouse with Ivy.

It was June, short dark hair and tiny little braid

over her ear and everything. It was the perfect drawing to help her forget about how horrible her birthday had been so far. It was the perfect drawing to remind her that tonight she was going to her first-ever dance with her first-ever crush as a first-ever teenager.

Right now June looked ready for her first-ever dance too. She grinned when she saw Ivy, a bright smile that Ivy would paint in pink and yellow starbursts if she could.

"Happy birthday!" June said, pulling Ivy into a hug. She smelled like violets. Or maybe lilacs. Something purple and pretty.

"Thanks," Ivy said, even though she didn't want to think about her birthday right now.

"Do they have cake here?" Taryn asked, craning her neck toward the snack table. "We need cake. You haven't had cake today."

"I don't need cake."

"Everyone needs cake," Drew said, coming up next to Taryn, who grinned at him.

"Hey, Drew," Ivy said. "How are you?"

He gave her a small smile and shrugged. "I'm okay, thanks."

Ivy could feel her best friend looking at her. Taryn

had been kind of quiet all afternoon while they were getting ready. She had shrieked over Ivy's dress, and Ivy had shrieked over hers—a pale pink thing that reminded Ivy of fairy wings—but that was really it.

June's hand slid into Ivy's and squeezed her fingers. Ivy's heart leaped and soared.

"Let's all go dance," June said, smiling at Ivy.

"Yeah. Dancing is good," Ivy said.

Then June grabbed Taryn's hand as well, while Drew mumbled something about finding his friends first.

"Ugh, boys," Taryn said, but she was smiling as she watched Drew lumber off toward a group of guys near the DJ.

The three girls headed toward the dance floor. Ivy could feel her palms sweating into June's as they got closer. Because this was it. Dancing. With June. Right here and right now, it was happening. Suddenly the gym felt like one giant treehouse, sparks of light and music and magic everywhere.

June pulled Ivy and Taryn to the center of the floor. A peppy song blasted through the speakers, and all their friends and even a few teachers were moving to the music. June and Taryn immediately started dancing, swaying their hips and lifting their arms in the air.

Ivy hesitated, wondering where she fit. June and Taryn were facing each other and giggling, but then June grabbed Ivy's arm and pulled her closer and soon the three of them were moving in a little circle. Ivy's dress floated around her legs, and the cool air spun between her hands as she waved them above her head. She smiled and laughed, and her friends smiled and laughed, and it felt exactly like her first-ever dance should feel.

Then the music slowed down. There was a nervous feeling in the air as kids coupled up around them, tiny smiles and eyes darting to the ground. Ivy slowed down too, her breathing heavy as she watched all the arms circling around waists and shoulders.

Boy-girl, girl-boy.

Ivy's mouth went dry. It went even drier when Drew clomped over to Taryn and asked her to dance. It went positively desertlike when Taryn waggled her eyebrows at Ivy and wove her arm through Drew's, leaving Ivy and June alone.

Ivy glanced at June, who was smiling as she watched Taryn loop her arms around Drew's neck. June's eyes sparkled, and everything about her seemed wistful.

They were surrounded by pairs of boys and girls, but Ivy ignored all of them and took a step closer to

June. She couldn't think about what people would say. She couldn't think about where she would put her hands—would she hold on to June's waist or would June hold on to hers? She could only think about June. And together, she was sure, she and June could figure out anything.

"Hey...June?"

June turned toward her.

Her eyes met Ivy's.

Ivy's met June's.

Ivy's hands were sweaty.

Her heart was like a jet plane, zooming around her body.

"So..." Her mouth was so dry that it nearly hurt. *Zoom, zoom.* "Do you want to—"

"Get some punch?" June said. "Yeah, I'm dying of thirst."

Zoom...crash.

"Oh," Ivy said. "Yeah, totally."

Ivy followed June as she wove through the dancers. Ivy's heart was dissolving in her chest. If she drew herself right now, she'd use all the watery blues, her whole solid body dripping and melting into a puddle like the Wicked Witch of the West.

"This is so fun," June said, still out of breath as she grabbed a cup of fluorescent red punch from the table and chugged it. Mr. Lowry, an eighth-grade math teacher, filled up more clear plastic cups. "Don't you think this is fun?"

"Yeah."

"I mean, a year ago? Never thought I'd get to go to a school dance. But look at me!" June held her arms out and sloshed a bit of punch on her wrist. "I mean, yeah, my mom's here, and she's probably spying on me from behind some plant right now with her stethoscope hidden in her pocket, but hey, I'm at a dance. I'm *dancing*. It's a miracle. And you and Taryn are spending the night at my house. Another miracle."

She babbled on, and Ivy nodded and smiled, trying to figure out what just happened. Didn't June want to dance?

"Now," June said, "if I could just find a boy to dance with, that would really make this whole night a dream come true."

Ivy blinked at her. It took a few seconds for June's words to sink in, and when they did, all Ivy could get out was a croaked "What?"

June swallowed another gulp of punch. "You know,

a boy. I love dancing with you and Taryn, but I guess I should try to slow dance with a boy. I'm almost thirteen. I'm supposed to have already danced with a boy, right? Do you think I should go ask one?"

"What...what do you mean, *supposed to*?"

But Ivy knew. Every doubt Ivy never let herself have about this dance was coming out of June's mouth right now.

Supposed to. Boys. Dance.

June didn't answer. She kept on talking, her normal stream of chatter in hyperdrive. "Taryn looks like she's having fun with Drew. I never thought I'd slow dance with anyone either, but now that I'm here, I should try it. I want to try everything."

If Ivy could melt any more, she would. She felt so stupid. It sounded so weird, June talking about boys. But it's not like she ever talked about girls either. Of course June wanted to dance with a boy. Of course June thought she was coming to the dance with Ivy as friends. Of course, of course, of course.

Ivy's eyes stung as she glanced around the room. "There's Charlie York." She jabbed a finger toward a cute, dark-skinned boy from her history class. "He's nice. Go for it." Her voice sounded flat and mean at the same time, the black gleam of a snake's eyes.

June frowned, but glanced at Charlie. "You think I should?"

Ivy forced herself to look at her. There was an eagerness in June's question that Ivy had never heard before. Her heart was no longer zooming. It wasn't melting or standing still.

It was shattering.

"Sure," Ivy whispered.

June wrapped both her hands around the empty cup so hard that the plastic crinkled loudly. "You really think I should go ask him? Like, really *really*?"

"I think you should do whatever you want to do," Ivy snapped. She couldn't help it. Her shattering heart was sharp, jagged pieces of glass everywhere.

"Okay, maybe I will," June said, folding her arms.

"Okay, good."

June frowned at Ivy, clearly confused, but she didn't move toward Charlie. Neither of them made a move to do anything. They just stood there, watching all the couples dance around them like they weren't even there.

---◄◄◄◆►►►---

CHAPTER TWENTY-NINE

Ivy's Keeper

J une had somehow convinced her mother to let Ivy and Taryn spend the night. Ivy dropped her new messenger bag full of borrowed clothes on the floor of June's room and slumped into a squashy armchair in the corner. June's room was pretty, all soft blues and greens with white wood furniture. If Ivy weren't feeling so rotten, she would've marveled over the gauzy canopy draped over the bed and how all June's books were organized by color.

But Ivy *was* feeling rotten, and so she said nothing about anything. And, of course, after the girls changed into pajamas, Taryn suggested they watch a movie about a big, dramatic high school dance.

June's mom set them up with all kinds of weird snacks like green bean chips and baby carrots with hummus and vegan carob-chip cookies. The three of them piled onto June's big bed, with June in the middle. She and Taryn giggled over the romantic drama, but Ivy couldn't force out even one laugh. It was all boys with girls, girls with boys. How was Ivy supposed to know how to handle all these feelings for June, all these feelings at all, if everything she saw and read about and heard about was all boy-girl, girl-boy?

Ivy started getting madder and madder at the whole thing. At June's dumb giggle. At Taryn's Drew this and Drew that. Ivy was so tired. She just wanted to go home. She wanted a birthday cake with her family, and she wanted Layla to sing "Happy Birthday" in French like she'd done every year since she started learning the language in eighth grade. But wanting all that just made Ivy angrier because she had no home and she had no birthday cake and right now, she might as well have no Layla and no family.

Ivy watched the lime-green alarm clock on June's bedside table tick over to 9:33. She'd been thirteen for eleven hours.

"What's wrong, Ivy?" Taryn asked. She threw a piece of natural, unbuttered, sea-salted popcorn at Ivy's head.

"Hmm? Nothing," Ivy said, tossing the popcorn back at Taryn.

Taryn lifted herself onto her elbow and peered at Ivy over June. "You're quiet."

"I'm watching the movie."

"Did you have a good birthday?"

Did. Past tense. It was over and done with. "Yeah."

"Was it weird, not being with your family?"

"It was fine."

Ivy could feel Taryn frowning at her. June was mercifully silent. The movie played on, but Ivy could tell no one was really watching it. Taryn was on a mission.

"Pondering mysteries?" Taryn asked.

"No," Ivy snapped. "I'm not pondering anything."

"What do you mean, 'pondering mysteries'?" June asked, but neither Ivy nor Taryn answered her. Ivy dared a glance at Taryn, who looked crushed. Ivy had never been so rude about refusing to play their game before. But Ivy didn't know what to say. She felt raw, a painting that wasn't dry yet. One hard nudge and she'd smear all over the place.

"What's going on, Ivy?" Taryn asked.

"Nothing is going on."

Taryn sat up and crossed her legs, ready for battle. "Do you know why I started the pondering mysteries thing?"

"Because you can't handle silence?" Ivy said.

Taryn frowned and shook her head. June was trapped between the two of them, her eyes fixed on the TV screen.

"No," Taryn said quietly. "I started it so you'd talk to me."

That made Ivy sit up. "What does that mean? I talk to you all the time."

"No you don't. Not about anything important. It's like, when we started middle school, you just...stopped."

"Since sixth grade? That's not true. I see you every day."

"Seeing isn't *sharing*. And then when I—"

Taryn pressed her mouth flat and lay back down.

"When you what?" Ivy asked.

"Never mind. You don't get it."

"Listen, Taryn, I do tell you stuff. I tell you about..." But Ivy couldn't finish that sentence. She knew she hadn't told Taryn about her treehouse pictures and liking girls, but she hadn't been this way since last year, had she? Then again, last year was when Taryn and all the other girls in school started talking about boys constantly. And Ivy never knew what to say anymore.

"Oh, like you told me all about how your parents forgot your birthday?" Taryn asked, and Ivy felt herself pale. "You think I haven't noticed?"

Ivy shook her head and looked away, embarrassed. Forgotten.

Taryn's own phone rang, belting out the theme song to Star Wars. She sighed and grabbed it from the nightstand.

"It's my mom. She'll want to hear about the dance." Taryn scooted off the bed and left the room, heading toward the bathroom in the hall without another word.

Ivy released a lungful of air. Taryn's mom would keep her distracted for at least ten minutes, so Ivy had some time to get her heart rate back to normal. Taryn shared everything with her mom. Right now she was probably sharing that Ivy couldn't seem to share anything.

"Did your parents really forget?" June asked after a

few seconds. On the TV screen, a girl and a boy plotted to set their best friends up on a date.

Ivy didn't answer her, just shrugged and kept staring at the screen.

"What's pondering mysteries?" June asked.

"It's a thing we do when we get quiet for a while," Ivy said without looking at her. "We tell each other stuff we find mysterious about the world or whatever we might be thinking about."

"Sounds fun."

"Oh yeah, a blast. Couldn't you tell?"

June inhaled at Ivy's sharp tone, but Ivy ignored her.

"I should've let you two talk alone," June said.

"It's okay."

"You don't seem okay."

Ivy gritted her teeth. The one time she wanted someone to tell her everything was okay, she got the opposite.

"You seemed kind of upset," June said. "Before now, I mean. At the dance."

June's voice was soft and sensitive. It infuriated Ivy. It made Ivy so mad that June didn't already know. It made Ivy so angry that she had to reveal this part of herself, that she couldn't just *be* and let that be okay and enough. It made Ivy so furious because if June didn't know, then that meant she wasn't Keeper. It meant Ivy had everything wrong, and she had no idea how to make it right.

But there was one thing she could do.

"You really want to know?" Ivy asked, but she didn't wait for June to answer before she was up and digging through her messenger bag for her yellow notebook. She flipped it open to the drawing she spent all afternoon working on.

She dropped the notebook on June's lap.

"Here. My letter to the world," Ivy said.

But as soon as she said it, as soon as her notebook left her hands, all her fury melted into nothing. She was bare and tiny, a girl standing in front of her first crush, confessing everything.

The drawing was one of her stormy drawings. Probably her favorite. The tree mimicked the sunset, all golds and oranges and lavenders and dusty pinks. The colors bled one into the next, making the tree look like a sky, pink apples bobbing from cloudlike leaves. Behind it, the real sky was the lightest blue and smooth, the kind of clear you got first thing in the morning.

Inside the treehouse, two girls stood facing each other, so close their noses were tip to tip. Both of their hands were laced together and held between them. There was no space between their bodies. Chest, hips, legs. They were complete comfort and peace. They were gentle sunsets after a storm. They were *together*, and it made Ivy blush from the tips of her toes to the top of her head.

It was so terrifyingly obvious, she wanted to rip the notebook out of June's hands. But June was holding it so tightly, her fingertips were white as she took in all the details.

One girl had soft pink hair, wild curls that had been left unbraided for too long. The other girl had a dark pixie cut growing out, a single braid plaited next to her ear.

One girl was Ivy.

The other girl was June.

And that was terrifyingly obvious too.

June blinked at the picture, her face completely expressionless.

9:46.

9:47.

"June."

June shook her head, like she was clearing it.

"June, please say something."

But June remained silent, staring at the picture. Ivy stood next to her, breathing in and out, but the panic was filling her up. June hated it. She hated Ivy for feeling it. Everything was falling apart, the treehouse branches snapping, the winds blowing.

"What's going on?" Taryn asked, appearing in the doorway. Ivy didn't say anything. She couldn't. She was trying to keep from crying, from screaming, from grabbing her secrets and running home.

Home.

A sob rose up in Ivy's throat, and she shoved her hand against her mouth to keep it inside. She reached for her notebook, and June let it go, her fingers limp. Probably from shock, Ivy thought. June finally lifted her eyes to Ivy's and they were wet.

Ivy had made June cry.

"I'm sorry," Ivy whispered.

"Ivy, I—"

"What is it?" Taryn asked again. She stepped closer and Ivy started to close her notebook, but not before Taryn grabbed a corner and pulled it toward her.

Ivy let her. It didn't matter anymore.

Taryn's eyes devoured the page. Ivy waited for a shocked gasp, an "Oh my God," anything, but Taryn didn't do any of that. Instead, she ran her hand over the picture and smiled.

She actually smiled.

Ivy frowned at her, but before she could ask what Taryn was thinking, Taryn told her.

"I knew June was the girl."

Something went cold in Ivy. "What...what do you mean?"

Taryn looked at Ivy. Her lower lip wobbled. June was silent, but tears poured down her face, both of her hands pressed to her cheeks.

"I...I just wanted you to talk to me," Taryn said.

"What do you mean?" Ivy asked again, louder.

Taryn took a deep breath and handed Ivy's notebook back to her. Then she went over to her own bag and pulled out a notebook.

A purple notebook.

"I still think you should talk to someone about it. Even if it's not me," she said. And then she offered the notebook to Ivy.

The purple notebook Ivy had lost.

Ivy stared at it like it would sprout wings at any moment. "You're Keeper."

Taryn frowned. "I'm ... who?"

"It was you. The notes in my locker."

Taryn swallowed, but she nodded. "I found the notebook that morning at the gym. It was on the floor, so I picked it up and—"

"But you weren't there."

"I was there early with my mom. We brought doughnuts for everyone, but I couldn't find you, and then I found this." She held up the notebook.

Ivy's mouth went dry. That morning in the gym, she remembered Layla mentioning that Taryn had been there, before Ivy and June came back from the library. She'd totally forgotten.

"Your name wasn't in it," Taryn went on, "but I knew it was yours. I knew and I—"

"And you didn't give it back to me?" Ivy's voice raised to a screech and Taryn flinched.

"I was in shock, okay? I couldn't believe it at first."

"Oh, because it's such an awful thing to like a girl?"

"No, Ivy, that's not it. Just listen!" Taryn's eyes filled with tears. "I was upset that you didn't tell me.

270

All this stuff in the notebook, it was obviously important to you, and I—"

"I wasn't ready to tell you!"

"But you were ready to tell June?"

June made a whimpering sound and covered her face with her hands.

"That's my choice, Taryn," Ivy yelled, tapping the purple notebook. "None of this was yours."

"But writing those notes with me helped," Taryn said. "And I'd wanted to talk to you for a long time about, well, how you *didn't* talk to me anymore. You think I want to babble on and on about Drew Dunaway all the time? I just couldn't think of anything else to talk about. And I thought that if I talked about him, maybe you'd talk about someone you liked or at least something that mattered to you. You never even talk to me about your family anymore. Then your house got destroyed, and you never talked about that either. I just thought writing to you without telling you it was me might be good for both of us."

Ivy wanted to argue, but she couldn't. It was true. But none of that mattered right now. All that mattered was that her best friend had betrayed her, her crush hated her, and nothing was her own. Nothing was right—not her friends, not her crush, not her drawings.

Ivy yanked the notebook out of Taryn's hands and grabbed her messenger bag. She stuffed both notebooks inside and threw the strap over her shoulder. She slipped her feet into her shoes.

She didn't look at June, and June didn't try to stop her.

She didn't look at Taryn, even though Taryn's deep sobs were all she could hear.

She just left.

It was time to go home.

—≺≺≺◆≻≻≻—

CHAPTER THIRTY

Ivy, Lost and Found

Outside, it was dark and warm. Ivy kept expecting June or Taryn to burst out of the house and follow her, but there were no footsteps behind her.

Ivy couldn't even hear her own footsteps as she ghosted over the sidewalk. That was exactly what she felt like. A ghost, like everything in her was slowly fading. Her family forgot about her, her best friend betrayed her, her crush...well...she wasn't exactly sure what June was thinking, but based on her silence and tears, it couldn't be anything good.

Ivy walked away from downtown, away from the inn. Twenty minutes and a few turns later, it got quiet. She could still hear the hum of cars, but mostly it was crickets and breezes through the tall grasses of the cornfields and the big front yards in need of mowing. It smelled like rain, and the wind had that full feeling to it, like it was bringing something with it.

Ivy kept walking until she saw a familiar gravel driveway. Turning onto it, she broke into a run, her bag bouncing against her hip. Her feet crunched the rocks, and she felt almost giddy because her feet had crunched the rocks of this driveway so many times before.

She was finally going home, to the last place where everything made sense.

The trees broke and opened into her front yard. It was so dark that Ivy almost didn't see it.

Nothing.

She saw ... *nothing.*

She knew her house was gone, but it had still been here, even if it was only rubble. Not even three weeks ago, it was here. She could look around and see familiar things.

Now it was really gone.

There was nothing left. No rubble, nothing. Just a giant pile of bricks and a big dumpster filled with junk near the oak tree that Ivy fell out of when she was six and broke her right arm. Where her house once stood was an empty hole, like a giant grave waiting to be filled.

She sank to her knees in the too-long grass. She saw the storm cellar doors, but other than that, her whole life was...dead.

It was a ghost, just like her.

The wind kicked up and blew her hair around. A few drops of rain started to fall, but she barely felt them because she was gone. She'd never been at her house alone before, but somehow this felt right. It felt exactly how this night should end.

She got up and went to sit under the big oak. Its trunk was wide and knobby, and its leaves kept her mostly dry from the rain. In the distance, thunder rumbled, getting closer every minute. She knew it was dumb to sit under a tree during a thunderstorm, but this felt kind of perfect too. Like she and the storm and her lost house all belonged together.

So she sat there and cried. She sat there and held her own hand, trying to feel her own skin against her fingers. Trying to feel real, trying to own something.

"Ivy!"

The storm was loud now, just like her crying, and Ivy thought she heard her name all mixed up with the wind, like it really was making them one. Even under the thick oak leaves, her shirt and hair were soaked. Her bag was tucked under her legs, protecting her notebooks, all she had left.

"Ivy!"

She lifted her head. Because that wasn't the wind and some cosmic connection to the storm.

"Ives!"

Ivy peered through the sheet of rain and saw a bobbing flashlight and a girl running.

Layla crashed onto her knees next to Ivy, kicking up mud and dead leaves. The flashlight spun on the ground, and she threw her arms around Ivy. Her secondhand raincoat was slick and smelled like cheap plastic.

"Oh my God, Ivy," she said, pulling back and pressing her hands on Ivy's shoulders. "You're here. Thank God, you're here." She dug her phone out of her pocket and tapped on it, her fingers shaking. "Dad, I found her. She's at our house. . . . No, the old house. . . . Yeah. . . . No, we'll meet you back at the hotel. Okay, bye."

Before Ivy could say anything or react at all, Layla's arms were around her again, her face buried in Ivy's hair. "Ives, what's going on? I've been calling you all day! Why haven't you answered your phone? It's your birthday."

Ivy started crying even harder and tucked her chin into Layla's shoulder. She didn't want to—she wanted to push her sister away—but she was so tired.

Until she saw Gigi hovering behind Layla, holding an umbrella.

"What is she doing here?" Ivy yelled over the wind, yanking back from Layla.

"What?" Layla asked.

"Gigi." Ivy pointed at her. "Why is she here?"

Layla frowned, and Gigi took a step away from them.

"Ives," Layla said. "She's helping me look for you. You wouldn't answer your phone, and Mom called Taryn's house. We didn't know you were staying the night at June's. We didn't even know you went to the dance. We had to hear it all from Taryn's mom and Dr. Somerset. Then your friends told us you'd left. Mom and Dad are out looking for you too. What's going on?"

"But you were mad at her," Ivy said, warm tears running down her face. Her voice sounded like she'd swallowed sand. "Before the storm, you were fighting.

I heard you fighting that night, and you haven't talked for weeks because Gigi likes girls and you're mad at her."

It all tumbled out. Layla's eyes widened, and Gigi's mouth fell open.

"Oh, Ives. You heard us that day?" Layla asked.

"I came to your room to show you something, and I heard you crying, and I didn't mean to hear it." Ivy was sobbing now. "But I did and I don't understand, and I hate you because you were mad."

"Ives." Layla put her hands on her sister's shoulders, but Ivy smacked them off. Layla sighed and glanced over her shoulder at a freaked-out-looking Gigi. "I wasn't mad because Gigi likes girls. I wasn't. I'm not."

"Then why? She was crying and you haven't talked in forever. I know you haven't. Not until the night Mom and Dad went out."

"No, we hadn't talked in a while. But not because of who Gigi likes. I was upset because..." Layla sighed and rubbed her forehead.

"It's okay, Lay," Gigi said. She knelt down next to Layla, shielding them all with her big umbrella.

Layla nodded. "I was a terrible friend to Gigi, okay,

Ives? I was mad because Gigi didn't tell me, and I heard it from some guy I barely knew. I was hurt that Gigi didn't trust me with that. Not because she likes girls."

Ivy blinked at her. "Really?"

Layla nodded. "But even that was wrong of me because . . . well, coming out is hard, and I have no idea what that's like, and I should've just let Gigi do it the way she needed to. It wasn't about me. I should've supported her no matter what."

Gigi reached out and grabbed Layla's hand. Then Gigi grabbed Ivy's too.

"Ives."

Ivy looked up into Gigi's brown eyes. "Why did this make you so upset?" Gigi asked. "The idea that Layla might not be my friend because I like girls?"

Layla curled a piece of wet hair off Ivy's cheek, tucking it behind her ear. It made Ivy cry even harder.

Ivy nudged her bag out from under her legs and took out her purple notebook. She flipped through the remaining drawings, all her explanations so clear. Layla and Gigi waited patiently, and Ivy was glad. She needed the time to look.

To see herself.

As she looked at all her stormy treehouse drawings, all those pictures with her tucked away inside with some nameless girl, she noticed something else. In between all the treehouses were other drawings too.

Drawings of things Ivy loved, like the little cape off the Gulf of Mexico where her family went the summer she was ten, water like a sapphire under the sun. Ivy remembered she'd used every blue she owned to make the sea look like that. There were drawings of delicate purple violets and bright yellow tulips; a sketch of Ivy's mother, pregnant belly full and round as she drew in her own notebook; Layla, her head thrown back and laughing; Taryn with that peaceful look on her face she got whenever she and Ivy pondered mysteries together; a stack of books with a cup of tea set on top; this very oak tree, as viewed from Ivy's old attic room; Aaron's and Evan's tiny hands reaching toward each other as they napped on a blanket in the living room; Ivy, her foot resting on top of a black-and-green soccer ball and her arms crossed, her expression triumphant.

There were dozens of pictures, drawings of the things that made Ivy happy, self-portraits, all the colors of her world, all the things that made her feel like her. Liking girls was part of that, but it wasn't everything. It was one piece in a bigger puzzle, and when you put all the pieces together, there was Ivy.

"This is me," Ivy whispered. She slid her notebook into Layla's lap. "This is me."

Layla didn't say anything. She just took Ivy's offered notebook, being sure to keep it protected under Gigi's umbrella. Then she turned each page, carefully and gently, taking her time on each drawing.

"These are beautiful, Ives," Gigi said, and Ivy felt herself smile.

When Layla was done, Ivy handed her the yellow notebook, open to the picture of her and June in the treehouse. Layla's eyes softened with recognition.

"That's why you've been so upset with me lately," Layla said. "Because you thought I'd be angry with you like you thought I was angry with Gigi."

Ivy's throat ached. "Yeah. I'm sorry."

"For what?" Layla said, gliding her hand over Ivy's hair. "That wasn't your fault, okay? It was mine."

"I should've just asked you," Ivy said. "But I was scared."

"I know. I'm really sorry, Ives."

Ivy slid her purple notebook back into her own lap. She flipped through the drawings again. They all looked different somehow. Different from even a couple of weeks ago. They were a little splattered with rain, and the storm around them bent the trees and shook the earth, but the drawings were safe. As she looked at them, treehouse pictures and all the ones in between, she didn't feel so stormy anymore.

She felt relieved.

This is my letter to the world that never wrote to me.

Suddenly, she knew exactly what Emily Dickinson had meant. It wasn't about whether or not June liked Ivy back, and it wasn't about Taryn or Mom or Layla or what anyone thought about who Ivy was. It wasn't about the world at all.

Emily still had things to say.

And so did Ivy.

CHAPTER THIRTY-ONE

Belonging

Mom curled up next to Ivy on the bed at the Cal- liope Inn. Layla was tucked in on Ivy's other side, her fingers moving slowly through Ivy's wet hair. Dad sat at the end of the bed, and he kept patting Ivy's leg under the pink-and-white floral quilt, like he was making sure she was still there.

Aaron and Evan slept in their little bassinets.

Everything looked the same as it did before Ivy left to stay at Taryn's. The room was a mess, all their hand-me-down clothes and toys and towels slung over the backs of chairs and piled on the desk. It smelled the same—like baby powder and toothpaste and pea- nut butter.

But everything was different.

Earlier, when Layla and Ivy got back to the hotel room, Mom and Dad attack-hugged both of them. Then Mom made Ivy change out of her wet clothes and tucked her into bed. When Ivy was warm and dry, her parents brought over a double chocolate cupcake with a candle sticking out of the top and a small wrapped rectangular package.

Ivy devoured the cupcake, and now the package was on her stomach, still wrapped.

"I really think you should open your present," Layla said, nudging the package with her knuckle.

Ivy didn't really care what was inside. It didn't matter all that much anymore, but she opened it anyway. The wrapping paper was sky blue and sparkly, so pretty that it was almost a shame to tear it.

But Ivy was glad that she did.

Inside was a pack of beautiful, brand-new, dream-come-true, dual-tipped brush pens, the exact same ones she'd lost in the storm. Ivy hugged them to her chest like a lovey.

"I missed our 10:33 date," Mom said quietly after Ivy hiccuped out her thank-yous.

"Yeah," Ivy said just as quietly.

"I'm so sorry, baby. I tried calling after lunch, but I know it's not the same. I know I messed up."

"Why did you forget?"

Mom sighed. "I don't have a good reason. It's been a lot to deal with, Ivy. The house and then Aaron getting sick, and everything felt off after we sent you to Taryn's."

Ivy frowned, wanting to believe that. Not that things had been hard, even though she knew they had been, but that maybe her family didn't feel like her family without her.

"Is Aaron okay?" Ivy asked.

"He's much better," Mom said. "He misses you."

"He does not," Ivy said.

"He does too!" Dad said, wiggling Ivy's foot. "You're the only one who can pull off a good enough monkey face to make him laugh. I've tried, trust me."

Ivy smiled, but her heart still hurt. She felt more like herself than she had in a long time, but did this new Ivy—the real Ivy—still fit with her family?

"That picture I found," Mom said. "The one you drew of all of us that I liked so much?"

Ivy swallowed and looked at her mother.

"That drawing is not perfect, Ivy," she said. "Not by a long shot."

"Mom, way to be harsh," Layla said, but Ivy squeezed her sister's hand.

"You don't think so?" Ivy asked Mom.

"Nope."

"What picture?" Dad asked.

Mom lifted a brow at her. Ivy pushed back the covers, messing up their Aberdeen pile, and scooted off the bed. She found her messenger bag near the sofa and took out her yellow notebook, flipping to the back. There, she removed a folded piece of paper and handed it to her dad.

He unfolded it, his forehead wrinkling up as he looked at it.

"No," he said. "Definitely not perfect."

"Why are you guys being jerks?" Layla asked, huffing through her nose.

Dad smiled and handed the drawing to Layla. She snapped it out of his hands, her eyes widening as she took in the details.

"Oh," she said, her eyes finding Ivy's. "No, this is far from perfect."

Ivy took the drawing back and looked at it. It was her family. They were all there. Except for her.

But now, she saw where she should go. Right next to Layla so that they were sandwiched in between their parents. Maybe Aaron should be in Ivy's lap so she could monkey-face him if he got upset. She looked at all the colors in her new brush pens, and she could see herself, pink-haired and maybe wearing her favorite green Beatles shirt that Layla had given her but was now lost. A girl could dream. Ivy was very good at dreaming.

It wouldn't be perfect. Ivy wasn't sure that perfect existed. Because this family stuff, this life stuff, it was messy. Maybe *perfect* was just another word for belonging. For feeling like yourself. It didn't mean things weren't hard. It just meant they were right. It just meant that eventually things would get better, and make more sense, that your heart wouldn't always feel so lonely.

It meant *safe*.

It meant *okay*.

Ivy found her purple notebook in her bag and placed it in Mom's lap. Layla reached out and squeezed Ivy's hand, and she didn't let go as their parents flipped through Ivy's life. Layla didn't let go as they turned the pages of Ivy's heart, as Dad teared up and Mom ran her hand over her drawings with a little smile on her face. Layla didn't let go when they looked at all the treehouse pictures, when Ivy explained what they meant to her, when her parents wrapped her in their arms, pulling Layla with them, and they were a big, perfect Aberdeen pile again.

-‹‹‹◆›››-

CHAPTER THIRTY-TWO

Resilient Ivy Aberdeen

The Kellerman Gallery was packed. Most of the town had shown up to see *Resilient Helenwood*, and all the artwork that usually hung on the walls was replaced with a cornucopia of colors and mediums, words and photographs.

Two weeks ago, after the Spring Dance and Ivy's move back to the Calliope Inn with her family, Mom helped her go through all her drawings and pick out the ones she wanted to submit to Ms. Lafontaine for the show. They chose ten treehouse drawings, along with a new drawing of Ivy all alone, which would be at the center.

Alone, but not lonely. In the drawing, she was standing on a green lawn that looked exactly like the yard she'd spent the past twelve years playing in and running through. Campouts and hide-and-go-seek. Picnics and cartwheels. Storm clouds rose up behind her, dark and threatening, but a powerful sun peeked through, sending coppery rays through the whole drawing. And Ivy was smiling.

When Ivy handed all the drawings over to her homeroom teacher, she told Ms. Lafontaine that they were supposed to be seen as one piece, one story. She laid out the drawings on a few desks and told her teacher how she wanted them displayed.

Unframed.

Ripped edges of the paper intact.

Water splotches and wrinkled corners left alone.

Pinned with thumbtacks in a circle, all those stormy treehouse drawings surrounding one strong, smiling girl.

A girl who was sure about who she was. A girl who wasn't afraid or ashamed, even if a time came again when she wasn't so sure anymore. Because Ivy knew that *wondering* was what life was all about. Wondering was how you found yourself.

Underneath the piece, one single white card would read:

My Letter to the World

Medium: Ink on paper
Artist: Ivy Aberdeen

Ms. Lafontaine loved it. The school's principal loved it, and the elementary and high school art teachers and principals loved it. Ivy didn't know if they saw what those treehouse pictures meant to Ivy. Maybe they just saw two good friends, a portrait of community and bravery and safety, while the world went wild around them. And that was okay because that's what the drawings were—dreams that got Ivy through a storm.

Now Ivy stood before her piece as the gallery filled up and up and up. People came by, tilted their heads at her drawings, and Ivy held her breath while they inspected all the little bits of her heart.

But in the end, it didn't really matter what they thought. Ivy loved each and every speck of color on those drawings, and that's all she really cared about.

Still, it was nerve-racking having everyone see so much of her, and she was glad when she spotted her mom's pale red head weaving through the crowd. Layla and Dad were right behind her, a baby boy strapped on each chest.

"There's my girl!" Mom said as she reached Ivy. Ivy threw her arms around her mom's waist.

"Looks like it's going well," Dad said, ruffling Ivy's hair.

"I think so," Ivy said.

"Duh, you're brilliant," Layla said, grinning at Ivy.

Ivy made a monkey face at Aaron, his feet dangling from Dad's carrier, and he giggled before stuffing his fist into his mouth.

"So proud of you, sweetheart," Mom said. "When we get settled at Jasper's mom's place, will you help me figure out my next Harriet story?"

"Really?"

Mom nodded. "Absolutely. And I think it's time for you to start writing your own stories too."

Ivy smiled. "Yeah. Maybe I will."

"June's piece is really nice," Layla said. "Have you seen it?"

Ivy's smile dimmed a little, and she shook her head. Ivy hadn't included the drawing of her and June in the treehouse as part of the show. The short-haired girl was very obviously June, and Ivy didn't feel right about putting it out there for everyone to see. For the past two weeks, Ivy and June hadn't really talked. Ivy didn't know if that was because of June or herself, but she pretty much avoided June, spending her lunch time in the library. June hadn't tried to talk to her either. Ivy wasn't sure there was anything left to say, and she guessed that was okay.

She guessed it had to be.

Ivy's parents said they were going to look at the other art pieces, and Layla met up with Gigi while Ivy hung around her piece. She was supposed to stay close to it in case anyone wanted to "discuss" it. It seemed weird to Ivy, the idea that someone would want to discuss her drawings.

It wasn't long before Taryn slid up next to her. She was wearing a gray dress with tiny pink flowers. Just as with June, Ivy hadn't talked to Taryn since the night of her birthday. Taryn had slipped a few apology notes into Ivy's locker, but Ivy never responded. She didn't feel mad, but she didn't feel *not* mad either. She felt... hurt.

They stood there for a long time, just looking at Ivy's piece.

"Pondering mysteries?" Taryn finally asked.

Ivy let herself smile a little. "Pondering a lot."

Next to her, Taryn exhaled. "How does ink come out of pens?"

"Parallel universes. Freaky."

"We only use ten percent of our brains."

"Area 51."

"Boys, ugh."

Ivy laughed, but then it faded quickly. "Friends."

Taryn's smiled dropped away too. "Those are a mystery."

"They shouldn't be."

"No, they shouldn't." Then Taryn turned and faced Ivy. "I'm so sorry. Taking your notebook and keeping it from you, writing you all those notes without telling you who I was, that was wrong. Really, really wrong, and I'm so, so sorry."

Ivy nodded. The hurt didn't go away, but she thought about Layla and Gigi and why Layla had handled everything so badly.

"I'm sorry I pulled away from you this past year," Ivy said. "I didn't know I was doing it, but you're right. I did. But I really wasn't ready to talk about it, Taryn. I wasn't ready because I was figuring it out. And even though I know that I like girls...well, I'm still figuring it out. Figuring *me* out. I'm not sure that ever goes away for anyone. It's a lot. But I need you to know it wasn't because I didn't trust you. It wasn't about you at all."

"I get that now," Taryn said. "I promise, I get it."

Ivy nodded. "Okay."

"Okay."

And it was. It wasn't perfect, but it was a start. Ivy knew that Taryn loved her just as she was. That was one good thing that Keeper had given them both.

"This is so good, Ivy," Taryn said after a few seconds, motioning toward *My Letter to the World*.

"Thanks."

"I mean, it really captures the whole surviving-a-storm thing, you know? With the messy paper and the ripped corners, and you standing in your empty yard looking all tough and confident. It's awesome."

Ivy widened her eyes at her best friend.

"What?" Taryn said, laughing. "I can be artistic. I get it."

"I'll never doubt you again."

Taryn smiled, but then her expression grew serious. "So...have you talked to June?"

Ivy turned back to her piece, sighing.

Then, without warning, Taryn curled Ivy into a hug. "You should talk to June," she whispered. "She's your friend, and you mean a lot to her. She told me so." And then she squeezed Ivy close one more time and wandered away. Ivy watched her join Drew at his piece. It was a collage of shredded roof tiles surrounding a red heart covered in barbed wire. But the heart was whole, no cracks in sight. Ivy had heard that his parents officially separated, but Drew seemed to be doing okay.

Funny, Ivy thought, all the things people could survive that they never imagined they could.

Her eyes took on a life of their own, drifting through the room. Ivy saw kids from her school, kids from her sister's school. She saw Layla standing with Gigi, who was holding hands with a tall blond girl. That must be Bryn. Next to her, Gigi beamed, practically glowing. If Ivy drew them right now, she'd use all primary watercolors, bright blues and yellows, but softly blended and with delicate lines.

Gigi caught Ivy's eye and smiled. She waved her free hand at Ivy, her nails painted to match a rainbow—red thumb, orange forefinger, yellow middle finger, green ring finger, blue pinkie. Ivy wiggled her matching rainbow nails back, and Gigi gave her a red thumbs-up.

But something in Ivy still hurt, and she couldn't help looking around for June. She looked for her everywhere. Yesterday, she shared a turkey sandwich in the inn's office with Robin and Jessa, who was visiting for the next couple of weeks, and told them the whole story. They exchanged one of those smiles grown-ups use when they think a kid is really cute but also really clueless.

"Definitely a crush," Jessa had said, crunching on a baby carrot. Her glossy hair fell into her eyes and she brushed it away.

"Oh yeah," Robin said, and Ivy huffed a lot of air through her nose.

"I know," Ivy said. "Now what do I do about it?"

Robin's smile turned serious, and she took Ivy's hand. "Honestly? Nothing. It'll hurt for a while, and then it will get better."

Robin said it would be okay.

And Ivy believed her.

"You just focus on you," Robin said, ripping off an edge of crust from her sandwich and popping it into her mouth. "Focus on friendship and feeling okay with yourself and proud of yourself. That's what's important right now."

Ivy knew Robin was right, so that was what she was doing. Still, when she saw June near Annie Demetrios's drippy neon painting of a ballet dancer in a leg cast, her stomach flipped and flopped and then started running a marathon around her body.

Then Ivy noticed June's own *Resilient* piece.

It was the glass girl. A big painting on a canvas, actually, but clearly a glass girl was at the center. She was just like the one June had drawn in Ivy's hotel room, but bigger and more beautiful. The girl was made of all the blues, and little sparks shot out from all her edges, shards of glass falling off and away. Ivy stepped closer and saw words spread out all over the canvas. Ivy couldn't see it clearly, but she was sure it was June's glass girl poem, cut up and pasted here and there. There were photos too, of ice skates and soccer balls, tubes of lipstick and red high-heeled shoes.

It was beautiful. It was June's perfect letter to the world. And Ivy wasn't the only one who thought so. Dr. Somerset stood right in front of the piece, one hand pressed to her mouth, the other on June's shoulder. June leaned into her mom, one arm wrapped around

Dr. Somerset's waist. They stood like that for a long time, and Ivy was glad. She was glad June's letter finally found its recipient.

But then June turned her head, catching Ivy staring at her, and Ivy felt her whole body flame up in a wash of embarrassment. She turned away so fast that she made herself dizzy and disturbed one of the drawings near the bottom of her piece. She busied herself with sticking the thumbtack a little tighter into the wall.

"Hey, Ivy."

Ivy swallowed and took a deep breath before turning around. "Hey, June."

June ran her eyes over Ivy's piece, a little smile on her face. "Wow, Ivy. It's so perfect. Really perfect. I can't imagine how it could be more perfect. I mean, I knew if you ever decided to do something for the art show, it would be great, but wow, this blows me away. So pretty. So totally you. I can't get over it. It's so—"

"Breathe, June."

She did, inhaling deeply. "Sorry."

"Don't be sorry, just don't pass out. And thanks."

June nodded, folding her arms and keeping her eyes glued to the wall.

"I saw your piece too," Ivy said. "It's really amazing. It looked like your mom liked it."

June smiled, but didn't look at her. "Yeah, thanks. She did like it. And we talked about it too. A little bit. I think we'll talk more. She said we would."

"That's great."

June nodded and they fell silent.

"Listen, Ivy, I'm sorry," June said after a few weird seconds. "About that night at my house. Your picture was so pretty, but I didn't know what to say and I—"

"It's okay," Ivy said. "You don't have to explain. You don't have to like the drawing." Her throat felt tight as she got the words out, but they were the right words. It wasn't June's fault that she didn't feel the same. It wasn't Ivy's either. It just was what it was.

"No, but I did like it," June said. "It was really beautiful, and the colors were perfect, and I really loved the way you drew me. It actually looked like me, and I looked happy and like I was really living my life. I loved it."

Ivy blinked at her. "Okay..."

June looked down at the floor and her lip trembled. "I don't want you to hate me."

"Me hate you?"

June nodded.

"June...I don't want you to hate *me*."

June's eyes found Ivy's. "I don't. Ivy, I swear, I don't. I'm just sorry that I can't...that right now, I don't..."

"No, no, don't be sorry." Ivy wanted to hold June's hand, hug her, something. Not because she had a crush on her, but because June was her friend.

"I just..." June took a deep breath. "I got sick when I was eight, you know? I never got to think about any of the normal stuff kids did. I never got to do the normal things. Sometimes, I feel like I'm still eight, still stuck in elementary school, like I'm always trying to catch up. There's so much I haven't figured out or done or even thought about, not like you and Taryn and everyone else has."

"I totally get that."

"I didn't even want to dance with a boy the other night. I wanted to keep dancing with you and Taryn and just be with my friends. I just thought I should want to dance with a boy, you know?"

Ivy nodded.

"But that's silly," June went on. "The only thing we *should* do is be ourselves, right?"

Ivy nodded again, but this time, she added a smile.

"You're my friend," June said. "My *best* friend. I love you, Ivy. I really do."

Ivy's heart exploded, a lightning bolt through her middle, a thunderclap in her chest. It was a beautiful storm.

"Even though..." Ivy swallowed hard to keep the lightning inside, because it really wanted to spill out of her mouth and ears and nose right now. "Even though I am the way that I am?"

June's eyes widened. "Totally. But, no that's not right either. Not *even though. Because.* Because that's you, right? At least, it's a part of you, and you are who I want as my friend." Then June reached out and took Ivy's hand, wrapping her fingers around Ivy's palm. She squeezed.

Ivy squeezed back.

-‹‹‹◆›››-

CHAPTER THIRTY-THREE

Home

One year later

The room smelled like fresh paint and the lilacs Mom had set on Ivy's brand-new desk underneath the tiny circular window. The ceiling was slanted, with dark wood beams cutting through the white.

Ivy stood in the doorway and smiled.

"What do you think, Ives?" Layla asked.

She scooted around Ivy and dropped a box labeled IVY'S WINTER CLOTHES onto a twin bed covered in a quilt decorated to look like splattered paint. Mom was right behind her, Aaron in her arms. Mom set him down, and he toddled over to the bed, grabbing the quilt and then cruising around to the footboard.

"It's perfect," Ivy said.

And it was.

Her little attic room, all her own again.

"This room is seriously cool," Layla said, walking around. "You have to let me crash here sometime." She ran her hand over the exposed brick wall. During the rebuild, Dad wanted to include pieces of the house they'd lost, so he insisted on using all the intact bricks he'd managed to save when they cleared the rubble. Now every room had part of their old life in it, part of their family history.

"No way, this room is mine!" Ivy said. Layla pulled her into a headlock and dug her knuckles into Ivy's hair. "Ow, quit it!"

Mom just smiled and wiped her eyes. She'd been pretty teary this whole week while they were moving stuff into the new house. It had been a tough year, but there had been a lot of good stuff too. They lived in Jasper's mom's guesthouse for a while, but then finally rented a bigger apartment just outside of town. Still, none of it was home. They belonged here. The walls might be new, but it felt the same. It felt like home.

Mom pulled Layla and Ivy to her and kissed the tops of both of their heads. They wrapped their arms around her back, and Ivy's fingers tangled with Layla's. Aaron got curious and waddled over to them, yanking on the leg of Ivy's jeans. Downstairs, Dad was unpacking the kitchen, plates and glasses clinking together. Ivy heard Evan babbling from where she knew he was set up in his high chair, stuffing his face with Cheerios.

They were all here. They made it and they did it together.

Still, Ivy couldn't help but glance at her bed, her messenger bag resting on her pillow. Her fingers itched and tingled.

"Okay, Layla, time to let Ivy get settled," Mom said, reading Ivy's mind. "You're still meeting June and Taryn at the ice rink, Ivy?"

"Yeah, in about an hour," Ivy said. "June is totally obsessed with learning a sit spin."

Mom laughed. "That is one busy girl. What was it last month? Swing dancing?"

"Square dancing. I never want to hear a mandolin again."

Mom and Layla both laughed and Ivy joined in. In the past year, June had dragged Ivy and Taryn through a myriad of activities, everything from synchronized swimming to knitting classes at the rec center. Last summer, when Ivy decided she really did want to go to soccer camp with Taryn, June went with them.

"We'll leave you alone until then," Mom said. She smoothed her fingers down the braid she had plaited into Ivy's hair that morning and winked.

"Ugh, fine, go hermit away in your little notebook world," Layla said, but Ivy knew she was kidding. Layla smacked a kiss on Ivy's cheek, and Mom swooped Aaron into her arms, and then Ivy was alone.

She looked around her new room. Late-spring sunlight streamed in through the window by her bed, covering everything in a citrusy glow. She plopped down on the mattress and unpacked her messenger bag.

She placed both her purple and yellow notebooks on the bedside table. They were full, the pages covered in drawings of Ivy and girls she didn't know, girls she did, friends and treehouses and oceans, baby brothers and sisters and dreams, but she still liked to keep them close.

Digging around in her bag, she found a brand-new notebook. This one was green and white, flowers swirling over the cover.

On its first pages were the beginnings of a comic,

the pages divided into squares and rectangles. The story was about a lonely girl named Ivy whose house got destroyed by a tornado. It was about how she and her family sort of fell apart, but came back together again. It was about a girl who was figuring out that she got crushes on girls instead of boys, who was figuring out how to love her friends and how to let her friends love her.

How to love herself.

When Ivy told her about the idea, Mom had called it a *graphic memoir.*

Ivy just called it a letter to the world.

Acknowledgments

I love all the characters I have had the privilege of creating, but Ivy holds a very special place in my heart. I'm so grateful to the team who helped me bring her to life.

Endless thanks to my agent, Rebecca Podos, who believed in my ability to not only write a middle-grade novel, but to write the kind of middle-grade novel we didn't see sitting on too many shelves. *Ivy* would not exist without you.

Thanks to my editor, Kheryn Callender, and the whole team at Little, Brown Books for Young Readers. Kheryn, your passion and love for *Ivy*, as well as the readers who need Ivy's story, was inspiring and life-giving. I'm so proud to work with you and can't thank you enough for helping me to make *Ivy* the best book it could be.

Thanks to the designers at Good Wives and Warriors for the absolutely amazing cover. I could not have asked for a more perfect representation of this book's heart.

To my critique partners, Lauren Thoman, Paige Crutcher, Sarah Brown, and Alisha Klapheke, thank you for the laughs, the wine, the queso, the friendship. Writing with you is twice as good and half as hard.

Thanks to Kathryn Ormsbee for the early read and voice insight.

To Parnassus Books and Stephanie Appell, thank you, as always, for your tireless work in getting books into the right hands, especially the right kids' hands.

To Craig, Benjamin, and William, thank you once again for seeing me through, holding me up, and being patient with the worlds I create in my head.

And finally, to you, dear reader. Thank you for reading, for being brave, for being you. I can't wait to read your amazing letter to the world.